No Way Out

It's a babysitter's worst nightmare. Rebecca thought she could trust the man to drive her home along with his three-year-old son. But they ended up prisoners in a remote cabin in the woods—with no way out.

Home Before Dark

A killer is stalking the streets of a small town. And Sara has to walk home alone after school, alone on a long, empty stretch of road. But this time, Sara is not alone . . .

Somebody Help Me

Over and over, Laurie heard the voice crying in the night. Calling out to *her*: "Please, help me!" But no one else heard the voice of the frightened child. Maybe it was just a dream—or a living nightmare.

Watcher in the Dark

Erin thought babysitting little Abby would give her a chance to relax. But then the phone calls started. Abby began screaming in her sleep. And Erin felt someone watching . . .

Don't Talk to Strangers

Ben and his mother moved into a quiet beach house to forget the past. But when Ben suddenly disappeared, his mother knew the nightmare had returned . . . with a vengeance.

Don't Walk Home Alone

Jessica remembered every detail of the accident—her friend's broken body . . . and the driver's cold, mocking face. He remembers Jessica, too. And he's waiting for the day she walks home alone . . .

PROMISE NOT TO TELL

BEVERLY HASTINGS

BERKLEY BOOKS, NEW YORK

PROMISE NOT TO TELL

A Berkley Book / published by arrangement with
the authors

PRINTING HISTORY
Berkley edition / September 1995

ISBN: 0-425-14945-5

BERKLEY®
Berkley Books are published by The Berkley Publishing Group,
200 Madison Avenue, New York, New York 10016.
BERKLEY and the "B" design
are trademarks belonging to Berkley Publishing Corporation.

PRINTED IN THE UNITED STATES OF AMERICA

10 9 8 7 6 5 4 3 2 1

To Susan Bailey Wright, with thanks;
and in memory of Pat Hilton

PROMISE
NOT TO TELL

PROLOGUE

"So what it amounts to is that you've been cheating me," the woman said. "Well, it's too late to call anyone tonight. But as of tomorrow morning, I'll make sure your clever little game is over." She stared at the man coldly for another long moment. Then she turned on her heel and started out of the room.

The man's eyes filled with panic as he watched her walk away. He had to stop her. Without thinking, he reached out—his hand closed over the jagged surface of the large chunk of quartz on the table. In two or three steps he was behind her. As she grasped the doorknob, he raised his hand and brought the heavy rock down on the back of her head.

For a moment he stood there looking down at her, aghast at what he'd done. Then he clumsily knelt beside her still form and felt for a pulse. But she was dead.

Well, there was nothing to be done for her now, he thought. His earlier panic had disappeared and a calm efficiency took over. He swept the Indian blanket off the back of the couch and wrapped it around the woman's body. Then he lifted it up, slung the awkward weight over his shoulder, and went outside.

The big Montana sky was filled with stars and a bright moon highlighted the large ranch house and its collection of outbuildings. In the nighttime silence nothing seemed to be stirring. Then the silhouette of a horse and rider emerged from behind one of the buildings and headed out into the open countryside. There was a large bundle slung over the horse's rump behind the saddle, and every few moments the man glanced over his shoulder to make sure that it was still securely attached.

He trotted toward a string of trees along the edge of a river that flowed through the valley, dismounting when he reached them. He unlashed a shovel from the saddle and began to dig. But the ground was hard, and after half an hour he had only managed to create a small indentation in the soil.

The change in light, as clouds blotted out the moon's brilliant glow, attracted his attention.

He looked up to see dark, heavy clouds rolling in over the mountains on the western edge of the valley. A storm was on the way.

Shaking his head in frustration, he retied the shovel to his saddle, remounted, and headed toward the mountains. Not far up the trail was the opening of a small cave, partially blocked by fallen rocks.

Dismounting, the man untied the blanket-covered bundle from behind his saddle and laid it on the ground. He pulled a few large rocks away from the mouth of the cave. Then he grasped the wrapped-up body and crammed it into the shallow space. A foot, still encased in a scuffed cowboy boot, slipped out from under the blanket, but he shoved it back and then began searching for more rocks. By the time the first drops of rain were falling, the cave's opening was completely hidden.

He climbed on his horse again. By now the rain had begun in earnest. He pulled his cowboy hat lower over his face as he urged the horse to hurry back to the ranch.

CHAPTER

ONE

"Welcome to Bozeman, Montana's, Gallatin Field. The local time is two twenty-five P.M., Rocky Mountain Daylight Savings Time," the flight attendant's perky voice told the passengers from Los Angeles. "Please watch your step when leaving the aircraft."

Julie Stone stuffed the paperback mystery she'd been reading into her shoulder bag and then opened the overhead bin above her head and yanked down her duffel bag. She shuffled along with the other passengers through the jetway into the airport.

It was a modern-looking building, but a whole lot smaller than any airport terminal she'd seen at home. Wood beams crisscrossed the high sloping roof above her head, and as she went down the escalator to the ground floor, she was amazed to see a flock of gigantic metal birds in flight suspended by wires from the ceiling. What were they—geese, ducks? All Julie knew was that they were really big.

Once she was outside, Julie plopped her duffel bag down on the sidewalk in front of the terminal building and looked around. Brown-green fields stretched out for what looked like miles beyond the parking lot. Then the flat land ended abruptly at the base of the mountains. The air here was breathtakingly clear—quite a contrast to the summer smog she'd been inhaling only a few hours ago in Los Angeles. And the sky, dotted with fluffy white clouds, was intensely blue, unlike the smoky gray she was used to.

A skinny guy with carrot-colored hair stood awkwardly outside the baggage claim area and looked at Julie. He liked her light brown hair curling around her face and the way her jeans and cowboy shirt clung to her slender figure. After a moment he picked up his own duffel bag and edged nearer.

Julie sensed someone standing behind her and, a little alarmed, whirled around. Growing up amid the tensions of southern California, she had learned to keep some space between herself and people she didn't know. By now it was almost an instinct and she didn't like feeling that she'd let someone get so close without her noticing.

The redheaded guy was wearing T-shirt, jeans, and sneakers. And like hers, his duffel bag was new. Then she realized that his bag sported the same yellow tag that hers did, with K BAR K RANCH emblazoned in large black letters.

"Hi," the guy said. "Looks like we're going to the same place," he added, indicating the yellow luggage tags. "My name's Josh Malone." Julie told him her name and then, giving her a wry grin, Josh asked, "So what did you do wrong?"

Obviously Julie didn't have a clue what he was talking about, so Josh went on, his voice taking on a sarcastic tone. "I figure every kid who gets sent to the K Bar K has done something wrong. I mean, a teen dude ranch? Give me a break. They don't want us out on the range; they want us off the planet. This is just as close as they can get and not go to jail." He paused and asked again, "So what bad thing did you do?"

Julie's eyes flashed with anger. "I don't see that it's any of your business," she told him hotly. What am I supposed to say? she wondered. That I guess what I did wrong was let my mom die and then let my dad marry a witch?

Josh blinked behind his wire-framed glasses.

"Sorry I asked," he said, a look of confusion replacing his earlier smart-aleck smile.

Regretting her nasty tone, Julie said, "Hey, forget it. I'm probably just in a bad mood."

An open Jeep pulled up to the curb and the good-looking young man behind the wheel called out, "You two waiting for a ride to the K Bar K?" When Julie and Josh nodded, he got out of the Jeep and came over to grab their duffel bags. He threw them into the back of the vehicle. "Howdy," he said, "I'm Nick. Hop in."

Nick's tall, lanky frame and soft smile were right out of a Hollywood western. Julie felt her face flush as she realized she was hoping his smile was especially for her. He opened the passenger door for them and then went around to the driver's side.

"Our jailer, I presume," Josh said under his breath. Julie shot him her most withering look and then took the front passenger seat for herself. As the Jeep pulled away from the curb Julie allowed herself a quick glance toward the backseat where Josh sat. The boy was staring down at the floor, looking almost as if he were going to cry. Serves him right, Julie thought, but she determined to be nicer to him from now on. He was obviously more easily wounded than his tough talk let on.

"So, Nick, are you the owner of the K Bar K?" Julie asked brightly.

He glanced over at her in surprise. "Gosh, no," he said. "I just work there." He gave Julie another soft smile and then returned his attention to the road.

Julie tried several more times to start a conversation with Nick. "How long does it take to get to the ranch?"—"Not long." "Well, what's it like?"—a shrug and then, "It's a job." "No, I mean, what's the ranch like?"—"Just a ranch."

The highway heading east from Bozeman sliced up through the mountains, leaving behind all vestiges of civilization. Then they were over the top and twisting down. Turning south, they drove into an expanse of flat land.

The broad valley was green and gold, filled with some sort of wild grass that grew everywhere. There were no other cars on the highway and the only sound was the splashing of a small river that meandered nearby. Off in the distance Julie thought she could see ranch buildings peeking out from beneath clumps of trees. Otherwise there was no sign of life anywhere and she wondered if maybe they actually had left the planet. It was beautiful, but it was so big and so empty.

At an unmarked crossroads the Jeep turned

right and bumped along a dirt road for about a mile before slowing. Another dirt road shot off to the left and above it was a wide wooden sign held up by two poles. The sign said K BAR K RANCH.

As they turned onto K Bar K property Julie thought about how hard her stepmother had worked on her dad to get him to send Julie away for part of the summer. "She'll love Montana," Martha had coaxed. "All that fresh air and sunshine—how could you deprive her? It sounds so wonderful I wish I could go there myself."

How could her dad have fallen for such cornball lines? Julie wondered. Of course her dad had been a pushover for Martha from the first moment she moved into the next-door town house. Julie had spotted Martha as a phony right away. All that sugary sweetness, the eagerness to help out by taking Julie shopping, the gourmet dinners—none of it fooled Julie for a minute. But it sure had fooled her dad. The next thing Julie knew, Dad was explaining to her how much easier their life would be with Martha in it. And then, of course, he married her.

Julie felt the sting of unshed tears when she thought of the wedding. It had been less than a year ago, and at the time she was sure things couldn't get much worse. But she'd been wrong.

Before long, Martha started her campaign to get rid of Julie for part of the summer. Brochures for all kinds of camps for teens began showing up in the mail. "Julie will have the best time," Martha kept saying.

"I'm going to hate it, and I already hate you!" Julie had wanted to shout. But she hadn't.

Angrily scrunching down a little lower in her seat, Julie glanced across at Nick easily steering the Jeep along the rutted road. Perhaps he'd sensed her looking at him. Anyway he flashed her a friendly look.

Julie sighed. With Nick around, maybe the next two weeks wouldn't be the worst ones in her life, but Julie still hated the way she'd been forced out of her own home to come here.

CHAPTER

TWO

Once they arrived at the ranch buildings, Nick bypassed the front entrance to the long, sprawling main house and parked near a door at its far end. A pretty dark-haired girl about Julie's age was just coming out.

"Hi, Hannah," Nick called to her. "Why don't you show these two where to put their stuff?"

Hannah shrugged, said "Okay," and turned back inside, leaving the door open behind her.

"Don't mind her," Nick told Julie as he lifted her duffel bag out of the Jeep. "I think she's still a little unhappy about being here."

Right, Julie thought, unlike the rest of us who are totally thrilled.

Just then a man emerged from the barn and called to Nick. "See you later," Nick said, and turned toward the man while Julie and Josh

picked up their bags and headed into the ranch
house.

This end of the house looked like it had been
added after the main part was built. It turned
out to be a roomy dormitory with a long center
hall separating the sleeping quarters. Hannah
stood leaning against an open door on one side;
a little way down on the other side of the hall
another door hung open. She waved Josh on
down the hall and then stepped back, ushering
Julie into the spacious room beyond.

There were pairs of beds at each end of the
room and each bed had its own low chest of
drawers topped with a reading light as well as
its own tall wardrobe for hanging clothes. It
could have looked like a motel room, but the
handmade quilts on the beds and the western
motif of the furniture gave it a pleasant, homey
feel.

"Take your pick," Hannah said, waving at the
three obviously unoccupied beds. "It's only going to be the two of us. I took this one because
it's closer to the bathroom."

Julie hadn't really noticed the closed door at
one edge of the far wall until then. The bed next
to that door was Hannah's, and for a moment
Julie considered taking one of the beds at the
other end of the room just to let Hannah know

what she thought of her less than friendly manner. But that's too mean, she decided. Besides, she'd much rather be in the twin next to Hannah than clear across the huge space all by herself.

The bathroom was similarly spacious, with four sinks all lined up like a fancy hotel ladies' room. This time Julie distanced herself from Hannah and put her minimal toiletries on the counter nearest the fourth sink. Hannah's stuff was spread out all over, and it looked as if she'd brought an entire cosmetics department with her. Where exactly is she going to use all that eye shadow? Julie wondered. We're out here in the middle of nowhere. I wonder if she brought along a prom dress, too.

Don't be catty, Julie admonished herself as she went back into the bedroom.

Hannah was curled up on her bed hugging a pillow to her chest, and when Julie walked over to her own bed to start arranging her stuff, Hannah rolled over and turned her back to Julie.

"When did you get here?" Julie asked, determined to be pleasant.

"Last night," was the two-word reply.

Julie stuffed the last of her clothes into the chest of drawers and slid her empty duffel bag under the bed. "Well, I'd like to look around. Want to come?" she asked brightly.

"Yeah, I guess so." Hannah's voice was muffled. "Hang on a minute." She jumped off her bed and zipped into the bathroom without even a glance in Julie's direction.

As she stood there listening to the sound of water running in the bathroom, Julie had half a mind just to leave. All the attempts at friendliness were of her own making and she wasn't getting much in return from the other girl. Oh, yes, this was definitely going to be a fun two weeks, Julie thought angrily. Then she glanced down at the scrunched-up pillow on Hannah's bed. It was streaked and smudged with mascara. Hannah had been crying.

When Hannah emerged from the bathroom, her face was scrubbed clean. Her smile was a little shaky and her bright tone sounded forced as she said, "Come on, let's go. I'll show you around."

They ran into Josh outside, and as if to apologize for her earlier rude behavior, Hannah made every effort to be friendly. As the three of them began to explore the ranch, Hannah told them what she'd learned about how the teen dude ranch got started.

It seemed that the ranch itself was very old. The original house had been built by the grandfather of the present owner, Mrs. Fremont. Her grandfather named the ranch the K Bar K for his two daughters, Katherine and Karen. Karen died as a child but Katherine grew up on the ranch, and when she married a local rodeo rider, he moved to the ranch, too.

Katherine and her rodeo rider had two children, a boy named Ned and a girl named Karen after her dead aunt. But Ned died in the last days of World War II, leaving his family with only their much younger child, Karen. When the child grew up, she married Jim Fremont and the couple made the K Bar K their home.

The Fremonts had one son, Jimmie Junior, and they encouraged their only child to have lots of playmates and visitors at the ranch. When Jimmie Junior got to be a teenager, they decided to add the dormitory wing just to accommodate his friends, and when he went back east to college, the K Bar K became known as the place to stay for summer break.

"So how come we're here instead of Jimmie Junior's kids and their friends?" Josh wanted to know.

"Because Jimmie Junior never had any kids. He got killed in a car crash after college," Hannah explained. "Mr. and Mrs. Fremont got lonely after that, I guess. They were used to having a bunch of kids around, so they started advertising for kids to come and stay here part of the summer. Then Mr. Fremont died and Mrs. Fremont is the only one left."

"How do you know all this stuff?" Julie wanted to know.

Hannah shrugged. "Oh, no one was around this morning except the weird twins and Roy, who is in a class of weirdness all by himself— you'll see what I mean when you meet him. So I found a booklet about the ranch and read it."

"The weird twins and very weird Roy," Josh mused. "They must be the other three guys in my room. I can't wait to meet them." He gave Julie a look that said plainer than words, "I told you this was going to be a lunatic asylum."

Julie laughed. Then she said to Hannah, "Well, aside from telling Mrs. Fremont how sorry we are for her loss, what else do we do for fun around here?"

"Do you ride?" Hannah asked. "We aren't allowed to take the horses out by ourselves, but maybe we can get Nick to take us out before dinner."

"Sounds like a plan to me," Julie told her, and the three of them headed for the barn.

But when they got to the barn, Nick was nowhere to be seen. Julie was disappointed, not so much about the ride as because it didn't look like she'd be hanging around with Nick for a while. Hannah shrugged and said, "Well, maybe he's off with the other two guys who work here. They have regular ranching work to do in addition to keeping us entertained."

They poked around in the barn and then wandered into the tack room, where Hannah spoke rather knowledgeably about some of the riding equipment that was stored there. Then she said, "The barn cat has a litter of new kittens. Want to see them?"

When it was time for dinner, the meal turned out to be a group affair with everyone sitting at a large table in the ranch-house dining room. There were eight of them: the six teenagers—Julie could see which were the weird twins, and weird Roy was every bit as peculiar looking as she'd imagined—and two adults Julie didn't know.

Where was Nick? she wondered. Then she guessed that he didn't live at the ranch like they did, but just came during the day. He was probably at home in some bachelor apartment eating take-out pizza, if they even had such a thing around here. She sighed. It would be a lot nicer if he ate with them at the ranch.

The man stood up and rapped his knife on his glass, interrupting her thoughts. "Hi, there," he said in a friendly tone. "I'm Gary and I'm what you might call the manager here. This is my wife, Ilene. Mrs. Fremont, the owner of the K Bar K, isn't well and won't be joining us tonight. However, she sends her warmest welcome and hopes you'll all have a marvelous time." He smiled at them and went on, "Normally Ilene and I won't be eating with you—Mrs. Fremont feels young people should be left alone without adults hanging around all the time."

To Julie his words sounded rehearsed. Then she realized that he probably said this same stuff to every new group.

"Since this is your first dinner together," Gary went on, "it might be fun if we go around the table and tell a little about ourselves." There was a group groan, but Gary just smiled. "Ladies first; let's start with you," and he looked directly at Julie.

I hate this, she thought. It's even worse than I imagined. But obediently she told them that her name was Julie Stone and she came from Los Angeles and that she was sixteen.

The others followed Julie's cue and introduced themselves with only name, hometown, and age. It turned out that they were all about the same age; Josh, probably feeling that they would look on him as a baby, stressed that he was almost sixteen. Hannah came from Connecticut, and the twins, whose names were Brian and Bret, came from near Youngstown, Ohio. Amazingly, both Josh and Roy came from the Chicago area, but that's all they had in common and it didn't look like they were going to be spending time together dishing hometown dirt.

Gary didn't look pleased with the recital and Julie wondered if he'd expected to hear them blab their innermost secrets. If so, he was doomed to disappointment.

Finally they were allowed to eat. They filled their plates from chafing dishes on the sideboard at the far end of the room and Julie suddenly realized that she was ravenous. She returned to her place with a plate piled high with pot roast, oven-browned potatoes, green beans that looked fresh from the garden, and a hearty helping of salad. As she took two warm rolls from the basket that was being passed, she decided that at least the K Bar K had one redeeming feature.

After most of them had scarfed down second helpings of almost everything, Gary rapped on his glass again. "I'm happy to see that you've done justice to Ilene's cooking," he began, and then he paused while they cheered for his wife, who stood near the sideboard smiling nervously. "All your meals will be served here. Ilene and Lucinda," he went on, indicating the shy girl who was clearing plates from the table, "will take care of the cooking and cleaning up." That brought more cheers.

"However"—Gary's voice rose above the din—"that doesn't mean that you won't be expected to participate in other helpful activities during these next two weeks. Breakfast starts at eight and I'll be over in the barn with Nick at nine o'clock to get you all started."

"What do you think he means by 'helpful activities'?" Hannah asked Julie as plates of cherry pie were being distributed.

Julie shook her head mournfully. "I don't think I want to know."

After Ilene and Lucinda cleared most of the plates and serving dishes to the kitchen, Ilene went over to say something in Gary's ear and then slipped outside. The rest of them were almost finished with dessert when Gary said in a surprised tone, "Well, look at this! Mrs. Fremont, how wonderful you could join us."

An older woman with her bandaged leg sticking out at the front of her wheelchair had appeared in the doorway between the dining room and the rest of the main house. Everyone at the table quieted down and turned to look at her. She smiled and raised her hand in greeting. "How nice to see all you young people," she said in a frail voice that sounded a lot older than she looked. "Gary has planned so many wonderful things for you to do and I know you'll all have a really happy time here at the K Bar K."

Not knowing exactly what was expected of them, the kids at the table clapped politely while Gary jumped up from his chair and went over to the woman. "How good of you to come in and say hello, Mrs. Fremont," he said solicitously.

"Well, good-bye, boys and girls," the woman said. "I'm sorry I can't stay longer." And with that Gary carefully turned the wheelchair around and gently pushed it out of the room.

Julie glanced across the table and saw Josh staring at her with raised eyebrows. "Weirder and weirder," his look seemed to say. Julie shook her head dismissively, but she, too, wondered if she'd been dropped into a different reality. It almost felt like the murder-mystery play she'd gone to in Los Angeles where you didn't know the script and couldn't tell who were actors and who weren't.

CHAPTER

THREE

After breakfast the next morning all six of the teen dudes trooped out to the barn to find out what kind of activities Gary had planned for them. Julie had suspected that "helpful activities" was really another term for "chores," and she was right. She wished she'd brought with her the K Bar K brochure, which referred to long trail rides and chuckwagon dinners and suggested that they'd all be hanging around the (nonexistent) pool between horseback rides.

There had been colorful pictures of kids splashing in a beautiful mountain lake and sitting around a cozy campfire while a cowboy strummed on a guitar. Now Julie wondered when those photos had been taken, and where. It was almost impossible to date scenic photos like those since there were no cars in them to give an idea of what year it might be and cowboy clothes never seemed to change style. And what she was facing now was not a mountain lake or a cowboy with a guitar next to a campfire. It was Gary, standing there trying to sell them all on the idea that painting the barn would be good for them and fun to boot.

There were other chores as well. Nick demonstrated how to saddle-soap the saddles and other riding gear. Gary assured them that they'd all be experts in no time. And it looked like they'd all be experts in pitching hay, washing and feeding the horses, cleaning the tack, and a whole host of other glamorous feats.

"Oh, yeah, this will be real valuable experience for me to use back home in Chicago," Josh muttered to Julie.

Julie gave him a wry grin, and Josh went on. "Yep, I plan to feature it on my college application. Maybe I can get into an agricultural school if I play my cards right."

Then they both looked at Hannah, who was staring down at her hands. Suddenly Julie realized what it was about Hannah's hands that she'd noticed earlier and couldn't put her finger on—Hannah had a professional manicure! Julie shook her head in sympathy—delicate, pretty Hannah was going to love this vacation.

Returning to his barn-painting theme, Gary

told them, "Your parents paid good money so that you could come out here and discover the beauty and wholesomeness of the west. They expect us to provide you with healthy outdoor activities, and in addition they'll be pleased to know that you are involved in a group project that requires a team effort and a lot of give-and-take."

Now Gary was really into his self-righteous explanation. "Working together to fix up this barn will give you something to strive for—a goal to reach and a success to savor. You'll get the chance to do it all, from buying the paint, which of course the ranch will pay for, to deciding among yourselves who's best suited to which part of the job. It's a splendid opportunity to get to know one another and to work together. I know you'll have a great time. Now, why don't you huddle together and decide who you want to be your team leader? Nick will drive you into town to purchase supplies once you've made up your list."

Six disbelieving faces stared at Gary. Julie noticed that Nick had disappeared out through the barn door during Gary's speech and she wondered what he thought of this idiotic idea.

There was a long silence while they mulled the situation over. Gary had the kind of determined expression that Julie sometimes saw on her dad's face. It meant, "This is the way it's going to be, like it or not." As she looked around she guessed that the rest of them had had similar experiences. She could almost read their minds as each of them wondered what would happen if they just said no. But none of them would be willing to try that alone.

They were like hostages here on the ranch with Gary in charge. If only they knew one another better, they could probably form some kind of group resistance. But singly they were afraid to speak out, not knowing if anyone else would support them. Even Roy, with a mutinous scowl on his face, was not uttering a word.

Finally Julie raised her hand. "Yes, Julie?" Gary said, giving her that phony adult smile.

"Do we only have to do one group project?" she asked. "I mean, if we finish the barn fast, can we just ride and stuff like that for the rest of the time?"

"Absolutely," Gary assured her. "You know, I'm not trying to be some sort of slave driver here. It's just that the K Bar K literature promises that you'll all be involved in one group project while you're here, something to encourage you to work things out with your peers and share the experience." He looked around to see if there were any other questions, and when no one else said a word, he started toward the door. "Okay. I'll leave you to it," he told them. "Find Nick when you're ready to go into town."

The hush that had fallen over the group continued for at least a minute after Gary left, then suddenly they all broke into speech at once. "If we're picking out the paint, let's get the most disgusting colors we can find," Josh suggested.

"Great idea," Julie said sarcastically. "Then we'd have to look at it the whole rest of the time."

"How long does it take to paint a barn?" Hannah wanted to know.

Brian and Bret, who so far hadn't uttered a word, looked at each other and then Brian said, "Well, we painted a fence at home last summer . . ."

"And it took forever," Bret said, finishing the sentence.

"But there are six of us," Julie pointed out. "It can't be that big a deal if we all get busy and get it done."

"Five," Roy corrected. "I ain't paintin' no barn. For sure my mom didn't send me here to learn to be a barn painter."

"Look," Julie insisted, "if we all work together I'm sure we can get it finished in no time."

Josh laughed harshly. "That's just what he wants us to do—work together. You're playing right into his hands."

Julie looked at him in exasperation. "So what do you suggest—that we stage a mutiny and sit on our hands for two weeks? You know he's not going to let us do anything fun until we get this stupid barn handled. Let's just get it over with."

"I agree with Julie," Hannah said, surprising them all. "Let's do it."

After a few moments Josh and the twins decided they might as well join in, leaving Roy as the only holdout. "No way. I'm not painting anything," he said again.

The five of them glared at him, but it was clear that Roy wasn't going to budge. Finally Julie said, "Look, Roy, you don't have to paint. Just go along with us and hang out looking busy so Gary doesn't notice that you're not doing anything. I'll do your part myself just to get it done."

"Sure, Roy, you just hang around and watch Julie do your share," Josh said with a sneer. "In fact we'll all do your share so you don't have to lift a finger. We wouldn't want you to have to actually do any work. You can just sit and watch us."

There was a long heavy silence. Roy gave

Josh a murderous look. Then he shrugged. "Fine," he said, giving the word a flat deadly quality.

After a moment Julie said, "Well, then, let's find Nick and get this show on the road." Quickly she headed toward the barn door, eager to escape the tension-charged atmosphere, and the others straggled after her.

It turned out that the ranch had a minivan to transport the groups of kids who stayed there. Nick got them all loaded inside and they set off on the road to town.

As far as Julie could tell, the town of Willow, Montana, didn't have one single willow tree, but the place was pretty cute anyway. She had half expected it to look like an Old West town from the movies, with hitching rails lined up in front of board sidewalks, and was a little disappointed to see paved streets, brick storefronts, and people wearing regular clothes. The town was also bigger than she thought it would be, with a dozen or so residential streets lined with houses, a small square hospital, and a downtown that had two banks and a movie theater advertising a new release.

Once she thought about it, she realized that the whole town had a population smaller than any single suburb of Los Angeles. But with all that open, empty space around it, the small town looked like a thriving city. I'd probably think two gas stations and a handful of houses were a big deal out here, she guessed, and then smiled to herself thinking what a difference perspective made. In Los Angeles, three empty lots felt like the wide-open spaces.

Nick parked on the main street and they all hopped out. No parking meters—now that really was something different. "Why don't you all look around and we'll meet back here at the van in an hour," he suggested. "The hardware store is over there." He pointed across the street. "We'll pick up the paint and stuff just before we leave."

Hannah already was eyeing a display of colorful handmade clothes in the window of a nearby shop, and with a wave to the rest of them, she went inside. Brian and Bret checked their watches and then ambled down the street, side by side. Julie was struck by how similar their actions were, especially as she watched them walk away. It was as if they were tied together with some kind of genetic tether. While she had seen them talking to each other, they had little to say to others, and when they did, they finished each other's sentences. How weird it would be to have another person so much like you, she thought. Would you think of your-self as a separate person, or would you always feel you were only half of a pair, dependent on the other half to make you whole?

While Julie had been watching the twins, Roy had slunk down an alley and now was out of sight. Julie had caught the movement out of the corner of her eye and wondered where he was going.

Now she and Josh and Nick stood on the side-walk near the van. None of them seemed ready to move. Josh appeared to be waiting to go wherever Julie went, and Julie was waiting for Nick. "Don't you guys want to explore the town?" Nick asked finally.

"Sure," Julie told him. "But I was wondering what you're going to be doing while you wait for us."

Nick shrugged. "Oh, just hang around, I guess."

There was something evasive in his manner, but Julie could see that he wasn't about to really answer her question. She turned to Josh. "Let's check out that boutique before Hannah buys the place out," she suggested. Then she strolled to-ward the shop with Josh trailing behind her.

The moment Julie entered the deep, shadowy doorway, she yanked Josh's arm and pulled him in near her. Holding her finger to her lips to silence him, she peered around the edge of the entrance and watched Nick turn and walk quickly down the sidewalk in the opposite direction. "I kind of knew he had someplace he wanted to go," she said to Josh, her tone sadly wistful. "He was just waiting to get rid of us."

"Think he's going to see a girlfriend?" Josh asked her.

Julie shrugged. "Who cares?" she said, but her attempt at nonchalance didn't fool Josh.

He tugged at her arm. "Come on, we'll follow him and find out."

"Are you nuts?" She stared at Josh in astonishment. "Isn't the guy entitled to some privacy?"

Josh laughed. "Not around me. I forgot to tell you, I'm Josh Malone, Ace Detective. Come on, let's go or we'll lose him."

Julie shook her head at Josh's attitude, but she went scurrying out of the doorway behind him and the two of them walked briskly after Nick, who was about a block away.

CHAPTER
FOUR

Nick's long strides ate up the pavement and Julie and Josh had to hurry to keep him in sight. He led them through the four-block business district and soon they were in a quiet residential area. The houses were a strange mix of tall, elegant Victorians and squat concrete-block boxes. Some had neatly tended lawns with clipped grass and borders of flowers, while others looked kind of junky, with ragged weeds, scruffy swing sets, and overturned tricycles in their front yards.

Luckily Nick never glanced back over his shoulder, because there were practically no other people on the sidewalks, no cars on the streets. Finally he approached an intersection with a huge gray stone building on one corner. It looked like an old school and you could see the edge of a play yard stretching out behind it.

Nick crossed the street and walked up the school's front steps. But instead of yanking open the door, he pressed a buzzer and waited. After a few moments someone inside opened the door and let him in.

Julie looked at Josh and raised her eyebrows. "What do you think?" she asked.

Josh shrugged. "Beats me. I never saw a school with a doorbell before. Maybe it's some kind of snooty place for rich kids where they won't let just anyone inside."

Just then they heard the noise of children and saw the flashes of moving bodies in the playground partly visible at the back of the building. "Come on," Josh said. "Let's take a look."

They edged around the corner so they were across the street from the school yard and partially hidden behind a large tree. They could see a dozen or so children playing with toys, all grouped close together in the middle of the yard, with three women hovering over them. The women almost appeared to be guarding the kids.

The kids were all different ages, from toddlers to some who might be about ten. And they didn't seem like rich kids to Julie. Instead of tidy uniforms or designer clothes, the kids were dressed in an odd assortment of what looked like hand-me-downs. And the yard itself certainly didn't belong to a rich school. There was no play equipment—just a level dirt field with a bit of patchy grass and two large trees.

"Well, if you were thinking of an investigative technique that included chatting up some of those kids when they played near the fence, you'll have to come up with a better plan," Julie told Josh. "It doesn't look like they're going to be left alone for a second. I guess we'd better head back."

"No way," Josh said. "We've followed Nick this far, we can't just leave. I want to find out what he's doing." He surveyed the building. "Maybe we can figure out another way to get inside and check things out. There's got to be an unlocked window or something."

"Josh!" Julie looked at him in alarm. "We can't just break in."

"Now's not the time to pull that self-righteous act with me," Josh said sternly. "You didn't seem to have a problem with following Nick here."

Julie was embarrassed. "Well, now we're here and I think we've gone far enough."

"You've got the hots for him. You wanted to see if he was going to meet a girlfriend," Josh said with a trace of malice in his voice.

Julie could feel her face flush. "Look, let's just forget it."

Josh shook his head. "You go back if you want to, but I'm going to find a way into that place."

"You'll get caught," Julie said. "No one likes someone prying into things. You could get in trouble."

"I never get caught," Josh informed her.

Julie wasn't sure if his bravado was just for her benefit or if he really was the class-A snoop he pretended. But she could tell from the mulish look on his face that he was determined to stay, overcome with his need to know. Well then, just let him do what he wants, she decided angrily.

The next moment she reconsidered. She'd gone along with him this far and now she couldn't just abandon him. Pictures of Josh setting off alarm bells at the school and a sheriff with a big badge dragging him back to camp and watching while he packed his stuff and took the first plane home flashed through her mind.

Julie looked at Josh and shook her head. She could tell there was no way she could talk him out of the idea of getting inside. But she certainly didn't want him breaking in. She'd have to think of another solution.

After a moment Julie said, "Okay. You want

to know what Nick is doing at this school." She paused and Josh gave her a challenging look. "All right, so do I," she admitted. "But no one is going around searching for unlocked side doors or trying to skinny through partly opened windows." With a gulp, she went on, "What we'll do is go right up to the front door and ring the bell."

"Are you serious?" Josh obviously wasn't used to such a straightforward approach.

"Sure, we can say we happened to see Nick come here and we wanted to ask him what time we're supposed to meet at the van or something."

Josh looked at her in disbelief. "You think anyone's going to buy that?"

Julie shrugged. "Well, I know it's a little lame. And if you can come up with a better story, fine. But I'm not leaving you here to break into that place and I'm definitely not going to do something like that myself."

"Okay, Ms. Honest and Upright. Fine with me. Lead the way," Josh told her.

Before she knew it, Julie and Josh were standing at the top of the school steps with Josh's finger pressed firmly on the doorbell. A moment later someone peered through the peephole at them and then a girl, a few years older than they were, opened the door. She looked at them suspiciously.

Josh prodded Julie with his elbow. He was letting her know this was her idea, and Julie could tell by his expression that he didn't think anything she said would get them in. "Uh, we're from the K Bar K," Julie explained haltingly. "We're staying at the camp there. I'm Julie Stone and this is Josh Malone. And, well, we wanted to ask Nick something."

The girl's face cleared. "Oh, hi. My name's Pauline. Nick is in the playroom working on the shelves. Come on in." Pauline opened the door wide and Julie shot a "so there" look at Josh before she stepped inside.

As Pauline led them along the school's central hall, Josh and Julie glanced curiously in through doorways on either side. The classrooms had been turned into some kind of dorm rooms with neatly made beds and clothes hanging from hooks on the walls. As they passed the stairway leading up to the second story, Josh said, "That's some serious-looking gate." The stairwell had been blocked off with heavy metal mesh that ran from floor to ceiling and as far up as the stairs had open sides. In addition, large padlocks ensured that no one was going to use those stairs in either direction.

Pauline laughed. "Oh, we only use this first

floor and we've got to be sure that the kids can't get on the stairs and get hurt," she told them. Then her face clouded over as she went on, "And we need to know that no one can break in upstairs and come down and get to us."

Wow, what is this, some kind of prison? Julie wondered. But before she could dwell on the question, they were being ushered into the old school's gym. It was small by Julie and Josh's standards, obviously built long before school sports drew huge crowds. The once gleaming hardwood floor was pitted and scarred, and if there had been bleachers at one side, they were long gone. Even the basketball hoop and its backboard were nowhere to be seen. What was left was a bare square room.

At the far end Nick was engrossed in attaching a set of low shelves to the wall. The raw wood looked fresh and clean next to the grimy walls that had long ago been painted a disgusting institutional green.

"Nick, your friends are here," Pauline called as the three of them walked across the room.

Nick looked up at Julie and Josh in surprise. "Am I late?" he asked. "I know I sometimes lose track of time. . . . " His voice trailed off as he glanced at his watch.

"Oh, I don't think so," Julie said, improvising

fast. "It's just that we couldn't remember when we're supposed to meet at the van. Anyway, why don't we help you now that we're here," she ended in a rush.

Taking the hint, Josh moved quickly to steady the set of shelves while Nick drove in the nails. Once it was secure, Nick stepped back and eyed it. "Well, there's nothing more I can do today," he said. "I'll let you know if I can come back tomorrow," he told Pauline. Then he nodded at Julie and Josh to follow him and the three of them walked toward the front door in silence.

"Good-bye, Pauline," Julie said with a smile. Pauline smiled a shy good-bye, then closed and locked the school door behind them.

Nick strode down the sidewalk, forcing Julie and Josh to practically run to keep up. He hadn't uttered a word since they'd left the school, and now they were into the main part of town. At this pace they'd be back to where the van was parked in minutes. Finally Julie could stand it no longer. "Nick, I'm sorry. It's all my fault. I was just curious, and when we saw you go into that school . . . I mean, it's summer and the place looked so deserted and run-down, almost like it was closed up. And, well . . ." she trailed off.

Although he'd slowed down the pace a bit,

Nick wasn't even looking at her. Julie felt her anger building. "Look, Nick, you may think it's none of our business, but that's no ordinary summer school. There's something strange going on there, and I think we have the right to know."

Nick stopped in his tracks and turned to Julie. "No, you don't. You were right the first time, it isn't any of your business. But you obviously figured out that something's a little odd, so I'm going to tell you. That abandoned school has been turned into a home for abused women and their children. All I was doing was helping out."

"Abused women and children!" Julie was shocked. She'd heard about places like that, but she'd never been inside one. "You mean, Pauline . . . ?"

"That's right," Nick said shortly. "But don't think those women want you sniffling all over them and acting sorry. They're just trying to get their lives back together and that's a safe haven for them until they can."

"But they can't be *living* there," Julie protested. "It's only an old ugly school building. It's disgusting."

Nick looked at her steadily. "It's the only place they have. A place where they can be safe and keep their kids safe. Not everyone has a nice normal home and new clothes and parents who are good to them."

Julie thought about her own family. She was still convinced that her stepmother was a witch who had only been interested in landing Julie's father for a husband. But certainly no one ever beat her up and even Martha was nice in some ways, taking her shopping and making sure the refrigerator was always full of Julie's favorite things to eat. The picture of her tidy home in the San Fernando Valley was juxtaposed against the reality of the bare, ugly rooms at the school. Julie shuddered.

Finally she said, "Can't we help? I mean, it's terrible to think of little kids living there. Isn't there something we can do?"

Nick softened slightly. "It's not all that bad. The town lets the shelter have the school rent-free and it even pays the utilities, so there's always water and light and plenty of heat in the winter. One of the churches donated a washer and dryer and some of the others give clothes and make sure the kids have toys to play with. And a couple of the civic organizations have food drives, so no one goes hungry."

Josh had been silent so far, but now he asked, "What are you doing there, Nick?"

Nick shrugged. "Well, I'm trying to fix up the

gym and turn it into a playroom for the kids. They need a nice place to keep toys and books and to play in when the weather is bad."

"From the looks of the playground, they need a nice place to play when the weather is good," Josh said.

Nick nodded in agreement. "You're right. All the playground equipment was dismantled and hauled away when they closed the school. I'm hoping one of the civic groups will raise enough money for new stuff, but play equipment is pretty low on the list of necessities."

"But you're going to need to do more than build shelves to turn that old gym into a playroom," Julie said, returning to Nick's project. "For one thing, the walls are disgusting. Whoever invented that color of paint should be shot!"

Nick grinned. "It is pretty repulsive, isn't it?"

"Hey, you know what?" Josh said excitedly. "Why couldn't we—"

Julie broke in. "I had the exact same idea myself!" She turned to Nick. "We're supposed to do some sort of camp project, right? But who cares about painting a barn. Why don't we use the money to buy paint for the school gym and paint that instead?"

"I don't know," Nick said slowly. "I'm not

sure Gary would like that."

"Who cares?" Julie waved that problem aside. "My dad paid good money for me to come here to the K Bar K and I think he'd much prefer I work on a shelter for battered women and children than paint an old barn on the ranch," she said defiantly.

"Sure, I know my parents would feel the same way," Josh told them. "And if Gary gives us any grief, we can tell him to talk to our folks."

"Besides," Julie added, "Gary's not the boss. And Mrs. Fremont seemed like a nice enough old lady. If she cares enough about kids to have them come to her ranch, I bet she'd love the idea of us helping some other kids who need it."

When they were about half a block away from the van, they could see the others hanging around on the sidewalk. Nick said, "I've got to make a stop here at the drugstore. You two go on ahead; I'll be along in a few minutes."

By the time they reached the van, Julie and Josh were still deep in discussion about how they would organize their project. And when they told the others about it, everyone but Roy was enthusiastic.

"I said I wasn't paintin' no barn and I ain't paintin' no gym either," he declared.

"Look, you," Josh began, ignoring Roy's

mounting hostility and clenched fists.

Julie quickly intervened. "Hey, knock it off," she told them both. "So what if Roy doesn't want to help. There's plenty of us to do it without him." She gave Roy a level look. "But, you will come into town with us and not let on to Gary that you're not working, won't you, Roy? You're not going to mess things up for the rest of us?"

"Nobody knows my business, least of all Mr. Gary," Roy told her.

"Well, what are you going to be doing while we're working at the shelter?" Josh wanted to know.

Roy glared at him. "I guess you didn't hear me. It's my business." Then he turned his sullen gaze on Julie and the others. "You don't need to worry. I won't mess up this thing you want to do." After a pause he added, pointedly including Josh, "And nobody better mess with me and my stuff either."

CHAPTER

FIVE

As soon as they arrived back at the K Bar K, Nick headed off in the direction of the barn to get the horses ready for their forthcoming ride. "He sure disappears a lot," Julie said, watching his retreating back. She was a little disappointed. She'd been hoping that her enthusiasm for helping the shelter, while genuine, would also bring about a closer relationship with Nick.

"I think he's a little bit afraid to be around when you spring this on Gary," Hannah told Julie. When Julie's face registered confusion, Hannah went on, "You know, this is Nick's summer job. He probably really needs the money and he could be worried that Gary will think this whole shelter business was his idea and get mad at him."

Julie looked at Hannah with renewed respect. Under that pretty, rich-girl facade, Hannah had a lot of common sense. "Then we'll make sure that it sounds like Nick had nothing to do with it. Besides, it wasn't his idea anyway."

When Gary tromped out of the ranch house, they all gathered around him. By unspoken agreement, Julie had become the one to explain things to him. It was as though she was trying to talk the principal at school into some new project, and she mustered up all her enthusiasm for the job.

But Gary was definitely not thrilled when Julie told him what they wanted to do. "You're going to use my money to buy paint and fix up that old school?" he bellowed.

Julie looked over at Hannah. The other girl's expression said as clearly as if she'd spoken, "No one promised this was going to be easy."

Taking a deep breath, Julie squared her shoulders. "You said you wanted us to have a group project, and that's what this is. Besides, it's not your money," she reminded him. "You're always telling us how much Mrs. Fremont wants us to have a good time. And I'll bet she'd love this idea." She paused and then said, "Maybe we should talk to her."

"No, no," Gary said hurriedly. "She's not feeling well and shouldn't be disturbed." A series of emotions passed across his face while he thought for a moment. Then he roused himself into looking as affable as he could. "Look, it's a fine project for you all, but I can't just let you go wandering by yourselves in town. I'm responsible for your safety."

"We'll be fine," Hannah said quickly. "And besides, we'll all be together, so what trouble can we get into?"

Julie noticed with satisfaction Gary's obvious mental calculations. It wasn't the plan he had in mind, but he was finding it hard to argue with them. She smiled at him. "Nick can stay with us and then you won't have anything to worry about," she added.

Finally Gary admitted defeat. Julie was ecstatic. Now they could do something really worthwhile, and besides she'd be spending a lot of time working with Nick. She crossed her fingers, hoping that Roy wouldn't let them down and that Nick wouldn't wonder about the absence of one kid. Thank goodness he hadn't been within earshot when Roy had said he wouldn't work at the school.

The afternoon horseback ride across the valley and a little way into the foothills was obviously meant to give inexperienced riders a feeling of confidence. "It's an easy trail, and a couple of hours this first time out is plenty,"

Nick told them as he helped them up onto their horses. "We don't want you too sore to ride tomorrow."

Julie had gone horseback riding a few times with her dad in Griffith Park, so she was sure she'd be able to handle things fine. It was only when she actually walked up to the huge beast she was to ride that she remembered that her riding experience had been years ago. Her horse's name was Maggie, a silky brown animal with a black mane and tail.

"We're going to do fine, aren't we, Maggie girl?" Julie crooned a little nervously.

"Don't worry about Maggie," Nick assured her. "She knows what she's doing. And if you ever get in trouble, just loosen your grip on the reins and yell, 'Maggie, go home!' and she'll bring you back here."

"Thanks," Julie said sarcastically, rolling her eyes. "Just what I wanted to hear."

It turned out that Hannah had been riding for years, but all her experience had been on an English saddle, so Nick reminded her not to try posting and just relax. "These western saddles are built for comfort," he explained. "Don't make it more difficult for yourself."

Nick led the way, and the other two men who worked at the ranch, José and Bob, trailed behind to make sure no one went astray. As Julie and Hannah rode side by side, their horses walking slowly, Hannah complained, "By the time I get home I'll be so sloppy in the saddle that I'll have to take lessons all over again."

Josh rode up to join them in time to hear her. "Yeah, I can see that would be a real hardship," he said. "Me, I'm just trying to stay on this thing."

Julie turned in her saddle to see Roy trailing behind them. His face was a pasty white and his hands gripped the saddle horn. Even his horse looked nervous, rolling its eyes and tossing its head from time to time.

"Roy certainly doesn't look like he's having much fun," Julie muttered to Hannah and Josh. The other two stole quick glances over their shoulders as Julie went on. "I wonder why he's here in the first place. He doesn't seem to fit in."

"No, he's a real city kid," Hannah said. "If he lived in New York, he'd be the one sliding through subway doors just as they were closing or riding a bike through midtown Manhattan traffic. I bet he'd like that a lot better than being out here in natureland with all these wide open spaces. But maybe his folks just wanted him to be more, uh, well-rounded."

Josh snorted. "Baloney. There's something

odd about him, something secretive. And I'm going to find out what it is."

"Well, he certainly likes to keep to himself," Julie admitted. "But, Josh, I think you'd be better off just leaving him alone."

Josh squared his slight shoulders. "I can handle myself," he told them. "Besides, I'm Josh Malone, Ace Detective, remember? I can find out anything."

Julie and Hannah looked at each other. Hannah's expression said, "Bad idea." Julie opened her mouth to try again to convince him, but at that moment Josh unwittingly kicked his horse and the animal broke into a brisk trot off across the field.

Before any of the others could react, Hannah gave her horse a kick and raced off across the field after Josh. By this time Josh's horse, sensing that its rider had lost control, was galloping in a wide arc that led back the way they'd come. The reins flew wild and loose, but Josh wasn't attempting to catch them; he was just trying to stay on.

Nick yelled at the rest of them to stop and Bob and José spurred their horses into action, cutting across the field in an effort to get in front of Josh's horse before it entered a little grove of trees they'd recently ridden through. Hannah reached Josh first as Bob and José came pounding up behind her. In one smooth motion, Hannah leaned over in her saddle and, grabbing Josh's flying reins, slowed his horse to a stop. Then, talking gently to both the horse and Josh, she turned and led them back to the group.

"Sorry, Nick," Bob called as the two men once again took up their positions at the end of the line behind Roy.

"You okay?" Nick asked Josh.

Now that everything was under control, Josh's bravado had returned. "Sure, I'm fine," he assured Nick. "Just wanted to get a little action going in this dull old trail ride."

Nick grinned understandingly. "Well, if you feel up to it, we'll keep going to the crest of the hill and then there's another way back down along the far side." He looked at Josh questioningly. "It'll take almost another hour to get back."

"No problem," Josh said.

"Good," Nick replied. "Now I think you'd better ride up front with me so I can keep an eye on you—one dose of excitement is enough."

Hannah handed Josh his reins, and while Josh and Nick rode slowly ahead she went to join Julie, who was still in line behind Brian and Bret.

"Why don't we just go back now?" Julie asked as soon as Hannah was close enough. "Josh is shaking like a leaf."

Hannah shook her head. "If Nick turned us around now, Josh's horse might try to bolt again. And even if he didn't, he'd figure that running off was the best way to end a ride early—horses are pretty smart. Besides, you've heard that old saying about getting right back up and riding after you've fallen off, haven't you?" Julie nodded. "Well, there's a lot of truth to that. Josh needs to know that he can keep going. He'll calm down once he knows he's got some control over his horse. By the time we get back, Josh will be telling all of us that he did the whole thing on purpose, just wait and see."

Julie laughed. "You're right, he will. But I bet he'll be stiff and sore tomorrow."

"For sure," Hannah agreed.

But Josh wasn't the only one feeling stiff after the ride. By evening Julie was certain she was walking with a barrel between her legs. "You need to soak in the tub," Hannah told her.

Julie wrinkled her nose in disgust. "I hate baths; I only take showers."

"Trust me," Hannah said as she turned on the tub faucet. There was a box of Epsom salts on a shelf in the bathroom and she threw a couple of handfuls of the white crystals into the water. Then she started rooting through the gigantic bag of cosmetics she'd brought with her. "I knew I'd packed this," she said with satisfaction as she pulled a tiny but expensive-looking vial of liquid from the bag. Hannah uncapped it and poured its contents into the tub, and soon mounds of delicious-smelling foam covered the surface of the water.

Julie recognized the fragrance. Her stepmother, Martha, had brought some home one day as a present. Later, at an upscale cosmetics counter in the mall, Julie had noticed that the scent came packaged as all sorts of things in addition to perfume and cologne—bath powder, body lotion, soap, and bubbling bath oil. And all of it was incredibly expensive. At the time she'd wondered who on earth would spend that kind of money on specially scented bath products; now she knew. But after soaking for half an hour in that gorgeous-smelling stuff, she had to admit it definitely had its uses.

Pulling the extra-large T-shirt she used as a nightgown over her head, Julie quietly opened the bathroom door, careful in case Hannah was already asleep. But the other girl was sitting on the edge of her bed rubbing lotion onto her elbows and arms. "Thanks, that was great," Julie said as she plopped on her own bed. "But I feel terrible using up that whole little bottle of bath oil."

"Don't give it another thought," Hannah told her. "My mom loaded me up with so much stuff for this trip that anything you can use will just be that much less I have to deal with."

"Well, thanks," Julie said. She got up, went to the old-fashioned mirrored bureau, and shuffled through her drawer for a moment. As she straightened up with a little notebook and pen in hand, she caught Hannah's reflection in the mirror. The other girl was watching her with an expression that was hard to read.

Then Hannah saw Julie watching her watch Julie and she blushed. "That's a great nightshirt," Hannah said.

Julie was surprised. She'd already noticed the silky, lace-edged nightgowns Hannah wore. They looked expensive and Hannah seemed to have a whole drawer full of them. She shrugged and returned to her bed, still clutching the notebook and pen. "Oh, it's just an old T-shirt of my dad's. He's a soundman for the movies and sometimes they make T-shirts that advertise the films. He always gets one for me in extra-large so I can use it as a sleep shirt."

"Wow," Hannah said softly, her eyes large.

"Your dad works in the movies? That must be great."

Julie grinned. "Yeah, it's a lot of fun sometimes. He gets me on the sets and I've met a whole bunch of actors." Then the smile faded from her face. "But every now and then he goes off on location and I don't see him for weeks."

It hadn't been bad before Martha, she remembered. When he'd had to go away then, often she got to stay with one of her girlfriends. Or there was this nice lady, Mrs. Sterling, who came to Julie's house. But now that Martha was on the scene, Julie was expected to be home with her stepmother. Thank goodness her dad had only been off on location once since he and Martha got married. But that one time had been bad enough.

Julie shook off the unhappy memory as she scrunched into a more comfortable position on her bed. Then she said to Hannah, "Look, I've got some extra T-shirts and you can have one if you want. They're really comfortable after they've been washed a few times."

"Are you sure?" Hannah asked. "I mean, we could trade." She leaped out of bed and snatched one of her delicate, frothy nighties from her bureau drawer. "Here, why don't you take this in exchange?" She thrust the shimmering item at Julie; the tags were still on it.

"But this is brand-new," Julie protested. "Mine are all used. I've worn them a zillion times. I mean, they're clean and everything, but . . ." She went again to the bureau and dug around until she came up with a T-shirt for a fairly recent movie. "This is the newest one I've got," she said as she gave the T-shirt to Hannah.

"Gosh, thanks," Hannah said. She disappeared into the bathroom. When she returned a moment later wearing her new sleep shirt, she stuffed the silky number into her dirty-clothes bag. "What do you think?" she asked.

"Great," Julie said with a laugh. She carefully folded her own new nightie and put it in her drawer. "I'll save this for sometime special," she explained. "Like when I go to a friend's house overnight or something." As she returned to bed she went on, "Are you sure you want to do this? I mean, won't your mom be mad? That nightgown looks really expensive."

"Don't worry about it," Hannah assured her. "It'll just give her an excuse to buy a replacement. Actually, I think one of the things she liked best about my coming here was that it gave her a reason to buy me a whole bunch of new stuff."

"Your mom likes to shop, huh?"

Hannah looked thoughtful. "No, I don't really think so. I mean, she loves shopping for me, but mostly she keeps saying how much she wants me to have everything she didn't get when she was a kid." After a moment she went on. "I suppose it's really the giving, not the shopping, she's into."

"Your mom sounds great," Julie said a little wistfully.

"Yeah, she and my dad are okay," Hannah said, but her voice had an odd tone. Then she asked, "What about your family?"

Julie opened her notebook and picked up her pen. "Oh, we can talk about them some other time," she said as casually as she could manage. "Right now I have to write a few lines in my diary and then hit the sack." She flashed a grin at Hannah. "Don't forget—we've got to get up at the crack of dawn."

"Yeah, I know," Hannah agreed. "It's as bad as being in school. I thought summer was supposed to be a vacation."

CHAPTER

SIX

The next day was just as bright and beautiful as the previous one. The sky was blue and cloudless and the dry air smelled slightly of sagebrush. "Is the weather always like this?" Julie asked Nick as they all climbed into the van.

He shook his head and laughed. "You should be here in the winter, or during one of our major rains. Besides, I thought you came from the land of sunshine."

"Yeah, I do," Julie said. "But it's never exactly like this."

"Clean air," Josh informed her. "That's what it is. Clean air always confuses city people like us."

On the way into town they discussed what they needed to buy to fix up the shelter. "White paint is the first thing on the list," Julie said. "That hideous green is so depressing."

"With maybe a little hint of pink in it," Hannah suggested. "That way it will be bright and cheerful even in the winter."

As usual, Brian and Bret had little to add to the conversation. But once inside the hardware store, they spent quite a while with the manager discussing the merits of various paint-roller covers and brushes before making a decision. In their own quiet way they, along with Nick, had somehow taken charge of the management of the project, leaving Julie, Hannah, and Josh to work out the look of the decor.

Roy, of course, contributed nothing. He skulked around the hardware store, picking up odd utensils and putting them down, and as much as possible acting as though he didn't even know who the rest of them were. At one point Julie, followed by Hannah, cornered him at the far end of the store. "Look, don't mess this up for the rest of us," Julie warned him. "Can't you at least pretend to be a little interested?"

Roy muttered something that sounded like a swear word, but Hannah gave him her best smile. "Roy, you'll be doing us a big favor if you can carry some of the stuff from the van into the shelter. Then you can do what you like until it's time to leave," she said coaxingly. "What do you say?"

He glanced at Hannah's imploring look and then down at his feet. "Well, okay. I'll help you as far as the shelter. Then I want you to leave me alone." This last was directed at Julie.

"Don't worry," Julie told him icily. "Just don't get into trouble."

Once at the shelter, Julie guessed that Nick had given everyone advance notice of their arrival. The kids were out in the yard with several of the women, the doors to the individual rooms were closed, and Pauline answered the door so fast that she must have been standing right there.

Pauline led them down the hall to the small former gymnasium, and with everyone carrying part of the load, it only took one trip to drag all the supplies inside. Roy did haul his share and even helped as some of them set up the paint equipment on one side of the room while others began organizing lumber for more shelves on the other side. Then Julie saw Roy and Hannah in quiet consultation near the doorway. A few moments later she looked around and Roy was nowhere to be seen.

"Where'd he go?" a voice asked in Julie's ear. She jumped and then realized that it was Josh, and he was also looking for Roy.

Julie said, "I don't know. One minute he was

here and the next he was gone. Let's ask Hannah—I saw her talking to him."

When they approached Hannah with their question, she shrugged her shoulders. "I haven't the foggiest," she told them. "He told me he'd done what he said he'd do and he was splitting, and that he'd be back before we left."

"And you just let him leave like that?" Josh sounded angry.

"What was I supposed to do, nail his shirttail to the wall?" Hannah replied sweetly. "Besides, we all agreed that he could do his own thing if he didn't cause any trouble for the rest of us."

"Well, I was planning to follow him and find out what he's up to," Josh said hotly. "And now he's disappeared. I don't think I can find him now."

"I don't think you should try to," Julie told him. "Just butt out, Josh. Leave him alone."

"No way. That guy's got a secret and I'm going to find out what it is."

Julie and Hannah looked at each other in exasperation. Then Hannah glanced around and said quickly, "Look, we'd better get to work or someone is going to wonder what's up and start counting heads. In the meantime, Josh, Julie is right—forget Roy or you'll get into trouble yourself."

"No I won't," was Josh's parting shot before he walked over to where Brian and Bret were pouring out paint into a couple of roller trays.

By the time three of the walls had their first coat of paint and the raw wood shelves had been built for the fourth wall, everyone was hot and sweaty and ready for a break. Eagerly they accepted Pauline's suggestion that they go out to the yard for some juice and cookies.

Julie noticed Pauline's look of concern as Hannah casually wiped her paint-stained hands on the legs of her designer jeans. "Will that paint wash out?" Pauline asked Julie.

Julie shrugged and grinned. "I don't know and I don't think she cares," Julie told her. And as Pauline continued to stare at Hannah, Julie went on. "Yeah, she's rich, but she's nice too. Don't let it get to you." She called Hannah over and introduced her to Pauline and soon the three girls were distributing the refreshments.

"Where'd the kids go?" Julie asked Pauline as she helped her pass out liquid-filled paper cups.

"The little ones are down for a morning nap and the older ones are having milk and listening to a story inside," Pauline said. "It's a little hard finding stuff to keep them occupied, cooped up in here like they are. But the moms manage somehow."

"You mean they don't leave at all?" Julie asked in amazement.

"Well, a couple of the women who've been here the longest are off at work. They got jobs waitressing in the hotel dining room and maybe they'll be able to leave before long. But the newer ones are too scared to go anywhere." Pauline sighed. "It takes a while. Before you feel safe enough to go outside, I mean."

Julie was dying to know what had brought Pauline to this place, but it was too personal to just come out and ask about. It seemed pretty clear that Pauline didn't have any kids. Julie certainly hoped not; Pauline couldn't be more than a couple of years older than she was, and without kids, maybe she'd find it easier to get out of here.

Before Julie could think of some clever way to get Pauline talking about herself, the other girl said, "Oh, Nick's glass is empty. Wait here and I'll run inside for another pitcher of juice."

Right, Julie thought. The rest of us could be dying of thirst, but when Nick looks ready, it's time to run and get more. A little annoyed at Pauline's obvious crush on Nick, Julie went over to where Hannah was sitting on the ground in the shade of the far tree.

"What a depressing place," Hannah said as

Julie sank down beside her. "There's nothing here but dirt. What do those kids do out here, make mud pies?"

"Yeah," Julie agreed. "It's too bad they carted away all the play equipment when the school was closed, but it probably was kind of dangerous. Those old metal things get pretty crummy after a while. I remember at my elementary school they took away the old slide after some little boy got hurt."

"Well, playgrounds don't have to be just metal equipment," Hannah told her. "There's lots of regular, old-fashioned stuff you can use to make a wonderful playground." She leaned her head back against the tree and closed her eyes. "When I was a kid, before we moved to the big house, we lived near this tiny community park. The dads had gotten together and used things they scrounged to build it on a little piece of public land. I guess you couldn't do something like that these days," she went on dreamily, "but it was a great place to play."

She sounds as though she was really happy then, Julie thought. I wonder what happened? Then something else clicked in Julie's brain. "What exactly did this little park have in it?" she asked.

"Oh, I don't know, some climbing stuff made

out of wood and a sandbox framed with railroad ties," Hannah said vaguely. "Why do you ask?"

"I was just wondering why we couldn't do the same kind of thing here." Julie's tone was casual, but there was a gleam of excitement in her eyes.

Hannah sat up straight. "I don't think so," she said. "First of all, Gary wasn't thrilled about paying for the paint for this place. He's not likely to go for playground equipment, too."

"But you said yourself that the play equipment you had in that park was made out of scrounged stuff. And we have more to work with than those dads did; we've got these great trees. If nothing else, we could get some long chain and a couple of tires and put up tree swings."

Julie's excitement was building and Hannah looked a little alarmed. "But where are we going to get things like that?" Hannah asked her. "We don't know anyone in this town. We don't even live here."

Julie laughed. "Oh, Hannah, I bet we could talk people into donating old items they don't need—they probably just haven't come up with the idea. Besides, Nick lives here. He'll know who we can hit up for stuff."

"I don't know," Hannah said doubtfully. "Besides, we still have the playroom to finish."

Julie waved that objection aside. "We'll be done there in a couple of days, the way we're going." She got to her feet. "Come on," she called to the others. "Rest time is over. Let's get to work." To Hannah she added more quietly, "We can talk to Nick later and let him start thinking about it."

When they ended the morning, all four walls had a first coat and the shelves were covered with primer. Roy appeared as if by magic just in time to help wash out the roller pans and clean the brushes. No one mentioned his absence and Julie wondered if Nick had noticed. Whatever he thought, Nick didn't say anything.

Lunch at the ranch was Mexican, and even before the kids filed into the rustic dining room, they could smell the tantalizing aroma. Bowls of refreshing gazpacho were set at every place and they lined up to help themselves to refried beans, rice, and homemade enchiladas. "I don't think anyone out here in the west has heard of cholesterol," Julie said as she squeezed another cheese-laden enchilada on her plate.

"Yeah, I know," Hannah said with a grin. "When I get home I'll be doing double time at the gym, but I'm sure enjoying myself now."

Ilene and Lucinda had cleared away the soup

bowls and everyone was enthusiastically tackling the main course when Gary ambled into the dining room. So far they hadn't seen much of Gary, and Julie figured it was just as well. He hadn't been very happy with them yesterday after he lost the argument about fixing up the shelter, and she wondered if he was the type to hold a grudge. If he was, he could make life on the ranch less than wonderful. But so far he'd been pleasant enough. He made brief appearances during some of the meals and was around when they saddled up for rides, and that was about the extent of it. Julie guessed that since he seemed to be in charge of the ranch, he was busy taking care of the real ranch work most of the time. If he planned to leave everything else to Nick, it was certainly okay with Julie.

Gary cleared his throat to get their attention. "Mrs. Fremont sends her regrets," he began. "She's a little under the weather, and while she usually visits a little with the kids who stay here, this time you won't be seeing much of her." It sounded sort of like a speech he'd prepared.

Gary took a breath and went on in a more natural tone. "We've got this end-of-session thing we do here that the kids all seem to like a lot. It's a solo one-day ride. By the end of next week all of you should be able to handle your horses with no problem, and you'll be familiar enough with the trails to find your way around by yourselves." He looked at the expectant faces around him. He had their undivided attention now. "So what we do is get you set up with a little packed lunch and you take your horse and go off by yourself. Everyone takes a different trail and you all meet at the summer hut up on the hill at dinnertime for a chuckwagon cookout."

"What are we supposed to be doing during the afternoon?" Josh asked suspiciously. He had visions of yet another unpopular project that Gary was secretly trying to get them to agree to.

Gary shrugged. "I don't know—anything you want. The idea of a solo is to be by yourself, on your own with nothing around you but your horse and the land."

"Wow, I think it sounds great," Julie said with enthusiasm. "But will we really be okay, by ourselves on the horses I mean?"

"Don't see why not," Gary said. "You can talk to Nick about it if you're nervous. But we've never had a problem yet, and a lot of the kids who come here are greener than you guys." He ambled toward the door. "Well, I just wanted to let you know what you have to look forward to," he added, and then he left.

Even before the door had closed behind him, there was a rising volume of talk about Gary's latest project. "Sure beats painting the barn," Bret said, and his twin nodded in agreement.

"A whole day alone, out on a horse. Sounds like heaven," Hannah said.

"You trying to tell us something?" Josh asked. "Don't I shower enough or what?"

Hannah's face colored. "No, no," she protested. "It's just that we're never alone, I mean really truly alone. There's always something— the phone, or TV, or other kids, or parents."

"I know what you mean," Julie agreed. "Won't it be exciting, sort of like cowboys in the Old West out on the range?"

"Probably just like cowboys out on the range in the new west, too," Roy added unexpectedly. "So, Julie, you gonna spend your time thinking great thoughts or what?"

Julie grinned. "I just might," she said airily.

Josh caught up with Julie and Hannah as they all headed toward the barn to start their afternoon ride. "Hey," he said. "I know you girls think this idea is great. You've got some romantic notion of riding off into the sunset and communing with nature. But what if someone gets lost or something?"

"Oh, Josh, you know better than anyone that

the horses run home to the barn." Hannah was teasing, but she could see Josh's angry look and she went on more kindly. "No one's going to get lost. The worst that happens is some of us end up back here and then start over to go to the summer hut."

Julie couldn't resist teasing him, too. "You're not scared, are you, Josh?"

"Of course not!" Josh said. "But you know someone like Roy could get hurt. He acts like he's never even been on a horse before."

"Oh, I'm sure they wouldn't do it if there were any danger," Hannah said reassuringly. "Besides, in a few days we'll all be riding as though we were born on a horse."

"Easy for you to say, princess. Easy for the rich girl whose parents have been giving her riding lessons since she could walk." Josh's voice was angry as he brushed by and strode off ahead of them.

"Oh, Hannah, he didn't mean that," Julie said.

"That's what all of you think, though. Isn't it?" Hannah said softly. Then she, too, lengthened her stride and moved ahead, leaving Julie to walk to the barn by herself.

CHAPTER

SEVEN

They were quiet on the ride. The angry words and hurt feelings had left their mark. Josh avoided both Julie and Hannah by riding with Brian and Bret. Hannah hung back, riding beside Roy. She seemed determined to be nice to the odd boy and to help him overcome his obvious fear of horses. Julie moved up beside Nick. At any other time she'd have been thrilled to be partnered with him, but now she felt totally left out, as though the only person willing to befriend her was someone who was paid to do so.

The ground rose sharply on one side of the trail, almost like a wall. On the other side was a gurgling creek edged with tall grass and wildflowers. Up ahead Julie could see where the trail narrowed to pass through a small canyon formed by two rocky hills. The silence in this

big land was intense. All she heard was the bur-
bling of the water and an occasional snort from
one of the horses.

Nick's horse moved ahead and Julie felt Maggie eagerly break into a trot to keep up with him.
But the rest of the group lagged behind, appar-
ently enjoying the beauty of the area and in no
hurry to catch up. As the two of them entered
the canyon Julie glanced at the tiny wildflowers
poking out from the cracks of the rock wall.
How amazing they can cling to such a barren
spot, she thought. Then a trickle of falling dirt
and small stones caught her eye.

Julie felt a small tremor of fear. The shower
of pebbles reminded her of the "Watch for
Fallen Rocks" signs on the Pacific Coast Highway back home. Do they have earthquakes in
this part of the country? she wondered uneasily.

Don't be silly, she told herself. In the next moment Julie gasped and automatically jerked
back on the reins as a large rock tumbled down
the canyon wall and landed just in front of Maggie's feet. The horse stopped dead and Julie
pitched forward in her saddle, clutching the saddle horn to keep her balance. Slightly ahead of
her, Nick looked back in alarm. Then his gaze
shifted up the rock wall, his eyes widening.

"Let's get out of here!" He wheeled his horse

around and grabbed Maggie's reins. "Stay back!" he yelled to the others who were approaching the beginning of the canyon. "Rock slide!"

Rocks and dirt were falling more rapidly now, and Julie felt a stone bounce off her shoulder. Nick pulled Maggie around and they started back, the horses skittering nervously past the mounting pile of debris on the trail. Julie clung to her saddle horn, her heart pounding with fear. Suddenly a jumble of large rocks careened off the canyon wall and jolted to a stop only a few feet in front of them, almost cutting them off from the opening of the canyon and the rest of the group.

"Hang on, Julie," Nick said, trying to sound calm. "We're going to get out of here just fine." Looking up apprehensively, he handed back her reins and said, "Just stay right behind me." He urged his horse through the narrow space between the pile of fallen rocks and the other canyon wall.

Nick looked back at Julie. "Come on, you can make it."

Maggie's neck was dark with sweat and she stood quivering, unwilling to go forward. Julie patted the big horse with a trembling hand. "Let's go, Maggie, girl. We've got to move."

Slowly Maggie took a few steps and then stopped again. Julie gave her a little kick and then whirled around in her saddle as she heard the clattering of another cascade of rocks behind her. "Maggie, come on!" Julie said forcefully.

The frightened creature seemed to make up her mind. She threaded her way around the pile of rocks, stumbling on the loose stones underfoot. Once they were through the narrow gap, Nick grabbed Julie's reins and both horses shot out of the mouth of the canyon. A roaring sound behind them made Julie look back; boulders almost as big as she was raised a cloud of dust as they tumbled onto the canyon floor.

As the horses milled around in a nervous cluster, Julie sat frozen in her saddle. Her whole body was shaking and the fingers of both hands were clutched tight around the saddle horn. Nick's horse stood so close that she could feel the warmth of its body against her leg.

"Are you okay?" Nick's voice was anxious.

Julie nodded—she couldn't trust herself to speak.

José said in an awed tone, "Man, I've never heard of that happening along here. Wonder what caused it."

"I don't know." Nick's face still looked pale,

but he made an effort to reassure everyone. "It's really unusual. But at least everyone's fine, and we'll keep to open country for the rest of this ride."

At the top of the canyon wall, a tall figure wearing a cowboy hat stood gazing down at the group of horses below as they started back the way they had come. He watched for a moment longer. Then, with a smile of satisfaction, he turned and walked toward the horse tethered to a small tree.

By the end of the ride, the terror of the rock slide had faded, and Josh was making feeble jokes about the dangers of the Wild West. Even Julie felt she'd be able to dismount without having her knees crumple. Nick's obvious concern about her made the scare almost worthwhile, she thought wryly.

As they arrived at the barn, a fancy new car was pulling up in front of the ranch house. A man in a western version of a business outfit—hand-tooled briefcase, bolo tie, cowboy hat, silver-tipped boots, and a soft chamois jacket hanging over his freshly pressed Levi's—got out and waved in their direction. Nick called, "Hi, Mr. Miller." Then Gary came out of the house and ushered the man toward the front door.

"Who's that?" Josh asked.

Nick shrugged. "Oh, Pete Miller is the town banker. I guess he must have some business with Mrs. Fremont."

"Well, I'm dying of heat," Josh said. "I'm getting some lemonade. How about if I bring some out for everyone?" Before they could respond, he was trotting off toward the house.

Josh entered through the screen door that led directly into the dining room and it slammed behind him as it always did. At home his mom was always yelling at him not to let the door slam, but here no one seemed to mind. Luckily, all evidence of lunch had long ago been cleared away and both the dining room and adjoining kitchen were empty.

Quickly Josh checked the refrigerator to make sure there was a full pitcher of lemonade inside. Then he walked quietly back through the dining room to the living-room area on the far side. This was where the kids sometimes hung out in the evenings, in front of the TV and a big crackling fire.

At the far end of the living room was a closed door, and beyond it lay the rest of the house. While no one had specifically told the kids they weren't supposed to go into that part of the house, it was pretty clear that it was off-limits. There was no way to get through from the dorm area; the kids had to go outside to get to the dining room. And they used the screen door that opened directly onto it from the outside, never going in the front door of the ranch house.

Josh listened at the closed door for a moment and then quietly eased it open. Beyond it was a large foyer with the front door to his right, a cozy den across the way, and a hall to the bedrooms running off to his left. He could hear voices coming from one of the bedrooms.

Taking a deep breath, Josh scooted across the foyer and tiptoed along the hallway. The first doorway he came to opened onto a big, airy bedroom. Josh guessed that the room would normally be flooded with light from the large windows across one side, but now the windows were shuttered and only a dim bedside lamp illuminated the room.

Mrs. Fremont lay propped up in the bed, her face in shadows. Gary and the banker were standing beside the bed. "But, Karen, I wish you'd think about this before rushing into things," the banker said. Then he looked at Gary with an embarrassed smile. "No offense intended, mind you, but as one of her trustees, the bank has certain responsibilities—"

The woman in the bed interrupted him, her voice feeble but insistent. "Maybe you'd feel better discussing this if Gary left." She made a shooing motion with her hand.

"You want me to go, Mrs. Fremont?" Gary asked uncertainly.

Josh panicked. He looked around for safe haven and decided that a closet across the hall was his best bet. He slipped into the small dark enclosure just in time. A moment later Gary clumped out of the bedroom and down the hall.

"Now, Pete, don't be difficult," the woman in the bed was saying as Josh eased out of the closet and closer to the bedroom door. "The bank does a fine job of overseeing my trust account, and I'm not suggesting a change in that. I only want to make sure that Gary and Ilene have unlimited access to my account once you put the trust money in it."

"I understand that, Karen, but—"

She cut him off again. "Pete, I don't want to discuss it further. I feel lousy, what with this awful cold, and besides that I sprained my wrist when I fell, and it hurts." Even Josh could see that her right wrist was wrapped in an elastic bandage. "I plan to do some traveling soon. If I'm out of town, or even if I'm just busy, Gary needs to be able to withdraw funds," she went on. "Did you bring that form with you for me to sign?"

The banker sighed and opened his briefcase, and Josh slipped back down the hallway and through the door to safety. What's that all about? he wondered.

He raced through the dining room only to be brought up short as he heard chopping sounds coming the kitchen. Oh, no, he thought. Ilene and Lucinda must be preparing stuff for dinner. He'd hoped the kitchen would still be empty.

Arranging his face in what he hoped was the picture of innocence and trying to steady his rapid pulse, Josh ambled into the kitchen. Lucinda stood at the counter cutting up potatoes and onions and adding them to the giant piece of meat in a nearby roaster. Ilene was nowhere to be seen. "Oh, hi," Josh said in his most casual voice.

Lucinda jumped and Josh realized that he'd startled her. Then another thought struck him: the people at the ranch no doubt liked the sound of the slamming screen door. It let them know when the kids were coming and going. He felt doubly fortunate that Ilene wasn't around. She'd have probably commented that she hadn't heard him come in.

"I just came in for some lemonade," Josh went on. "I want to take it out to everyone at the barn."

Lucinda smiled at him shyly and went on with her chopping. In another moment Josh, loaded with a pitcher of lemonade and a stack of paper cups, was slamming the screen door on his way out.

The rest of the kids were brushing their horses while Nick cleaned and put away the gear. "It took you long enough," Julie said to Josh as he approached. "What'd you do, pick the lemons first?"

"Ha-ha," Josh said. "As a matter of fact, Lucinda was working in the kitchen and she wanted my opinion about dinner tonight. I told her that I like lots of carrots and onions and potatoes in pot roast. Hope that's okay with you." He handed Julie a cup of lemonade and then poured some for everyone else.

As Hannah took the full paper cup he handed her, she gave him a funny look. "So Lucinda wanted your opinion about pot roast, huh?" she asked.

Josh blushed. "Well, we were just chatting. She's a nice person."

"Yes, she seems to be," Hannah said mildly, but she continued to look at Josh with speculation.

Having finished with Maggie, Julie wandered into the barn and plopped down on a bale of hay. Nick looked up from his work. "Are you sure you're feeling okay now?"

His voice was full of genuine concern, and at any other time Julie would have loved it. But right now, she realized, I don't want to think about what happened. "Oh, I'm fine," she told him brightly. Changing the subject, she went on, "You know, that playroom for the kids at the shelter is really coming along. It's going to make a terrific place for everyone to hang out at night and during bad weather, sort of like a rec room or something."

Hannah came into the barn as if on cue. "Yeah, the playroom is fabulous, Nick," she said. "And it's so great to watch the transformation, seeing that horrid room turn into something attractive and useful." She paused to put her brush neatly back on the shelf where it belonged. "It's really too bad about the yard outside," she said wistfully. "I doubt it'd take much of anything to fix it up, too."

Nick looked from Hannah to Julie and back to Hannah again. "Now, wait a minute," he began.

Hannah and Julie both smiled sweetly at him. "Just listen a minute," Julie suggested. "Hannah has an idea that wouldn't cost a cent."

The rest of the group gathered in the barn as

Hannah sketched out her plan.

"You can really, like, *make* a swing?" Roy interrupted as she was talking about hanging a tire from a limb of one of the big old trees.

"Sure," Hannah told him. "And it wouldn't need to be an old tire. If we had a piece of wood that was all sanded and finished and some sturdy bolts, we could hang a real swing from a couple of chains."

"No kidding," Roy said in amazement.

Josh looked at Roy with disgust. What right did he have getting involved in this? He hadn't done squat on the shelter project so far, except carry a few things. Josh thought Hannah and Julie ought to tell Roy to just shut up and butt out, but instead everyone seemed to welcome his enthusiasm.

"How about a plain wooden ladder held up by posts at both ends?" Brian suggested.

"Like a bridge that the kids could climb on and hang from," Bret added.

Nick held up his hands. "Wait a minute. We're not getting involved in concrete post footings and complicated stuff like that."

Julie smiled as she heard Nick say "we" and silently thanked Brian and Bret for their suggestion. It didn't matter that it wouldn't work; the important thing was that Nick was now clearly hooked by the project. "If monkey bars are too tough for us to handle, what about a barrel or something the little ones could crawl through? And there must be some way we can use one of those giant tractor tires. I'll bet it wouldn't be too hard to get someone to donate an old one, would it, Nick?" she asked.

"Well," Nick said slowly, "I guess I could ask around." His stern look included them all as he went on, "Just as long as you're not thinking of something bigger than we can handle in the next week or so. I don't want those women at the shelter to get their hopes built up and then have it left half-completed and totally unusable."

"Oh, no," Hannah assured him. "After all, we want to get the good out of seeing the finished product." She crossed her fingers behind her back so that only Julie could see them. "I can guarantee you that the playground will be all done in time for us to have a party there with the kids before we leave."

That night as they were getting ready for bed, Julie said to Hannah, "You went a little far out on a limb promising Nick the playground will get finished before the end of next week. I mean, what if it's not?"

"Well, it will be," Hannah told her. "We'll just

have to make sure of it." She grinned at Julie's worried expression. "Look, the worst thing that happens is we only make a few of the things we're planning. Then we'll stick in a bunch of plants and it will look gorgeous."

"Okay," Julie said a little doubtfully.

"In fact, that gives me an idea," Hannah went on. "I don't see why we can't dig up a small section of that yard and turn it into a little garden."

Now Julie was inspired. "Of course. That whole playground is nothing but dirt, and parts of it get good sun all day. A few bags of mulch or something should be enough to get a strip of soil in good shape. Then we can take seedlings from here when they thin out the vegetable garden—they'd just throw them away otherwise, so it's not like it's a big deal." Julie smiled at a far-off remembrance. "My mom and I had a vegetable garden when she was still alive. I loved spending time with her working in it—it was so special."

"You know, we're not in southern California here," Hannah reminded her. "The plants are going to die in the winter."

"So?" Julie countered. "That will just give them all something to start over together next spring." She grinned at Hannah. "This is going to be great! Even Roy sounded interested this afternoon. What's with him, anyway?"

"Oh, I think part of it is that he feels like he's odd man out, like he doesn't really fit in," Hannah told her. "I certainly know how that feels."

"Come on," Julie said. "You're practically running this whole show. And everyone likes your ideas. I can't imagine you feeling left out or different."

Hannah gave Julie a wry smile. "Maybe that's because I can be who I really am here—we all can. No one comes with preconceived notions about anyone else. It's like we were all dumped on Mars or something—no past, no future, just now."

Julie watched the other girl's retreating back as she disappeared into the bathroom. What a funny thing to say. But now that she thought about it, Julie had to agree that Hannah was right. There was something very freeing about being at the ranch. It was as if all that stuff from home simply didn't exist anymore and you could be anyone you wanted to be.

The image of Nick's face floated into her mind. What kind of person did he see her as? She felt pretty sure that he liked her, at least a little. And she hoped he was impressed with the ideas she'd come up with for the shelter and her persistence in getting Gary to agree. The trouble was that she never seemed able to spend any time alone with him. There were always other kids around.

"What do you think about Nick?" Julie asked out loud. The question had just popped out of her mouth as Hannah emerged from the bathroom, and she could have kicked herself for actually asking. But now that the question was out there, she waited for Hannah's response with interest.

Hannah grinned conspiratorially. "He sure is cute," she said instantly. "And I think he likes you."

Julie almost groaned. Was she that obvious?

"He kind of reminds me of one of the guys at home that I hang around with. In looks, I mean," Hannah went on. "But Larry, the guy at home, is real trouble with a capital T." She looked lost in thought for a moment and Julie saw the sad expression on her face.

"Is Larry your boyfriend?" Julie asked.

Hannah snapped back to the present. "Oh, no. Not anymore. In fact, I'm staying strictly away from him when I get home." Hannah made it sound like a pledge she'd made. Then she went on, "I'm sure Nick isn't like that at all. He seems really nice."

Julie watched Hannah as the other girl snuggled down in her bed and switched off the bedside lamp. I wonder if Josh was right all along, Julie thought as she switched off her own lamp and lay there in the dark. Maybe we were all sent here because we did something wrong. It certainly sounded like Hannah had gotten into some kind of trouble, something that had to do with a cute guy named Larry.

CHAPTER

EIGHT

The next morning at breakfast Hannah made a point of stopping Lucinda as the young woman was going back toward the kitchen. After a brief conversation, Hannah brought her plate over and sat down next to Julie. "Just as I suspected," she said in a lowered voice. "Josh is up to something. He lied about having a chat with Lucinda when he took so long with the lemonade yesterday."

"How do you know that?" Julie asked.

"Because I just tried to talk with her and she hardly said anything."

"Well, maybe you're not as appealing to her as Josh is," Julie said with a grin. "Who knows, that boyish charm of his may have started her rattling off nonstop."

Hannah shook her head. "You don't get what I'm telling you. It isn't that she doesn't want to talk to us. But she can't—she speaks very little English. Unless Josh has linguistic skills we don't know about, their conversation couldn't have been more than about ten words long."

On the way to the shelter Julie made a point of sitting at the back of the van next to Josh. The others were involved in a discussion with Nick about how the solo ride would work. Julie leaned over and spoke to Josh. "What exactly were you doing at the ranch house yesterday afternoon?" she asked, her voice low and insistent.

Josh blushed and ducked his eyes. But then his sense of bravado took over. "I told you I'm a detective. I find things out."

"Josh," Julie said warningly. "Don't mess around. It's not nice and it's not smart."

"I can take care of myself," he told her. "I like knowing secrets, and I plan to find out plenty before I'm through. For instance, I'm definitely going to figure out what Roy's up to when the rest of us are working at the shelter."

"Why don't you just leave him alone?" Julie suggested. "He sounds like he'll help out in fixing up the playground, so maybe it's just painting he hates. And there could be a million reasons for that. Maybe he's allergic to paint and doesn't want to say so. Who knows. Besides, he's not bothering you."

"He's got a secret and I'm going to find out what it is," Josh said stubbornly.

But once again, Roy helped carry stuff into the shelter and then disappeared before Josh realized he was gone. "Couldn't you have just kept him here talking for a few minutes?" Josh asked Julie angrily.

"Oh, Josh, forget it," Julie said with a sigh.

The introduction of the final outing alone gave new direction and purpose to the ride they took that afternoon. Instead of mindlessly following Nick on whatever route he took, the kids asked him questions non-stop. How did he know where he was going? What landmarks did he use? What if they got lost? And of course, what were the chances of another rock slide?

Julie felt a shiver of dismay at the question. She wanted to put the rock slide out of her mind entirely, and she resented the other kids' reminding her of the danger she'd so narrowly escaped. Still, she listened as Nick explained that he'd gone up to look at the canyon's edge. "I saw where the rocks fell, but I couldn't figure out what made it happen. But I'm sure there won't be another one. They're usually caused by heavy rain, and then it's only farther up in the mountains."

Nick went on to remind them that the solo ride wasn't some sort of endurance test but a chance to be alone with yourself, without the distractions of other people and everyday life.

"That's going to be some change for the twins," Julie said to Hannah later. "I'll bet neither one of them has spent a whole day by himself in his entire life. I wonder what they think of this 'adventure alone'?"

Hannah shrugged. "Who knows. They certainly seem enthusiastic, but with them it's difficult to know. I think they have one form of communication between themselves and another for everyone else."

At dinner that night Gary wandered in with another surprise for them. "The rodeo will be here this weekend, and Mrs. Fremont has managed to get tickets for you on Saturday night," he announced. "We'll have dinner a little early and then go into town. I want to remind you that even though it's warm during the day, it gets chilly at night, so take layers to add after the sun goes down. Nick will be on duty and arrange the transportation." He smiled as he heard their yips of enthusiasm and then went on. "And"—he paused for effect—"there's a street dance in town after the rodeo!"

The kids broke into excited chatter—a real

western rodeo and a big party in the middle of town afterward! Julie and Hannah grinned at each other, the identical thought flashing across their faces. What to wear?

It was lucky for Nick that he lived at home with his mom and didn't spend the evenings working at the ranch. As it was, the next morning he was peppered with questions about the rodeo and street dance as they drove into town.

The group wouldn't be working at the shelter over the weekend, and since this was Friday, Nick felt it might be a good day to scrounge up what they could for the playground so they could both start that and finish the details of the indoor project on Monday. Julie and Hannah decided they'd try tackling the feed-store owner about mulch and stuff for the garden while the guys hit the lumber mill and the hardware store. Then they'd drive to Nick's house at the edge of town. It turned out that his mom had already started gathering items from friends and neighbors.

Nick parked the minivan on Main Street and they all scrambled out. "Let's meet back here in an hour or so and see how we're doing," he told them.

Big banners strung across the streets announced the upcoming rodeo, and the town had already started to take on a festive feel. As Julie and Hannah introduced themselves to the smiling owner of the feed store, Julie thought, Nick is so smart. All the merchants were looking forward to a weekend of lots of activity and big sales; they were in an expansive mood, more willing than usual to help out a local cause.

At the lumberyard the guys were looking over the odd collection of freebies to see what they could use it for. After a few minutes Roy sauntered out of the yard and walked down the street. Josh, who had been watching for just this disappearing act, followed him. Suddenly Roy ducked into a store entrance, and when Josh approached the doorway, Roy stepped out and glared at him. "Where are you going?" Roy demanded.

Josh recovered from his surprise and grinned maliciously at Roy. "The real question is, where are you going? What are you up to?" He stepped in front of Roy to block the other boy as he edged into the alley beside the store. "I want answers, Roy. What's your dirty little secret?"

Roy flushed an angry red. "Stay away from me," he warned. "And stay out of my business!"

"You gonna try and stop me?" Josh taunted.

In a flash Roy's fist popped into Josh's face, knocking him down. For a gangly, skinny kid,

Roy's punch packed quite a wallop. "I'm warning you," he growled at the redhead lying in the
dirt near his feet. And with that, Roy fled down
the alley and disappeared around the corner.

Josh got up slowly and rubbed his face. Just
you wait, he thought. He brushed himself off
and looked around, thankful that no one had
witnessed the embarrassing incident. Then he
walked somewhat painfully down the street to
the soda shop; he deserved a treat. In the shop's
cool interior Josh sat on a stool at the marble
counter, sipping his ice-cream float and wondering what Roy was doing that was such a secret.

The group met back at the minivan gloating
over their successes. Hannah and Julie had not
only got the promise of bags of mulch and fer-
tilizer from the feed-store owner but he'd also
given them several long lengths of heavy chain
he had lying around. There was certainly
enough for two swings.

At the lumberyard Brian and Bret had had an
animated conversation with the foreman about
some kind of climbing rig they could put together, and they'd all come up with a design that
would be easy to do and require little more than
the odd pieces the man could give them and
industrious use of sandpaper. The man also told

them where he felt sure they could get one of those huge wooden cable spools that would become a sturdy picnic table.

"What happened to you?" Julie asked Josh when she saw the swollen lump on his cheekbone. Josh muttered something vague about not looking where he was going and running into a door, but when Roy showed up, she noticed that he and Josh stayed as far away from each other as possible. She could see Nick giving both boys an odd look, but he didn't say anything. Julie guessed that Nick might think things would work themselves out better if he left them alone and didn't make a big deal out of it.

The house where Nick still lived with his mom during college vacations was a large, comfortable place with big shade trees and a gorgeous garden. Nick's mom, whom she insisted they all call Etta, worked in the local real-estate office; she had taken an hour off so she could meet the group and tell them what she'd rounded up for them.

"I talked to Ralph Wiggs," she told Nick. Then she explained to the rest of them, "He runs a small ranch out on Route 32. Anyway, he's willing to give you an old tire from his tractor and he'll even deliver it to the shelter on Monday if you want him to."

"Fabulous," Julie said. "Now if we can get some clean sand . . ."

Etta grinned at her. "Oh, don't worry about that. I figured that's what you kids wanted to do with the tire, so I got Henry down at the highway department to send over a truck with a small load of sand. He'll have his men dump it near the gate to the playground on Tuesday morning. Probably it'll be there at the crack of dawn, but all you need to do is carry it in. And be sure to get a big tarp to cover the sandbox—you don't want a bunch of neighborhood cats to think you've provided them with a fancy new bathroom. Maybe Henry's got a tarp lying around, too. I'll call on Monday and ask him."

She passed out lemonade and cookies and went on, "It's wonderful what you kids are doing for the shelter. I mean, it's not even your town and you're putting in so much effort. Makes me ashamed that we haven't done more ourselves."

"Your mom is really nice," Julie told Nick as they drove back to the K Bar K. She'd wangled the front passenger seat next to him and was doing her best to pretend it was just the two of them alone in the minivan. "It must be great to have a big house and a mom like that to go home to." Nick shrugged agreeably. Julie went on,

"But you ride so well that I would have thought you grew up on a ranch."

Nick looked a little sad. "I did grow up on a ranch, at least till I was ten. Then my dad died and my mom sold the ranch and we moved to that house in town."

"Gee, I'm sorry," Julie told him. "What happened? To your dad, I mean?"

"Well, he started losing weight, and by the time he went to the doctor the cancer was already everywhere." Nick paused and went on, "They said they wouldn't have been able to do anything even if he'd been checked out sooner. He died a month later."

"Oh, my gosh, that's terrible," Julie said. They sat in silence for a few moments and then Julie said wistfully, "And your mom never married again. It was just the two of you together after that."

"Yeah," Nick said, and Julie was surprised that he didn't sound totally happy about it.

"You wouldn't have wanted your mom to marry someone else, would you?" Julie asked, responding to his tone. "I mean, no one could take the place of your dad."

Nick looked at her in surprise. "Of course no one could be the same as my dad. He was my dad. But sometimes when I was younger I wished there were a man at home—you know, to take care of us and do stuff with me and like that. I think my mom would have been happier, too."

"Did she have any boyfriends?" Julie wanted to know.

"Sure, lots. But she said she wasn't going to entrust the raising of her child to some other man, so she shooed them all away when they got too serious." Nick's eyes took on a faraway expression. "I wonder if she regrets that now."

"Of course not!" Julie protested. "Your mom's got a great life. She seems really happy."

"Yeah, probably, but I still worry about her. There she is in that big house all by herself while I'm away at school." He paused and then added, "Sometimes I've thought it would be fun to go off with my friends when they're planning something during school break, but then I think of my mom here alone and I just give it a pass. I don't think I would have gone so far away to school if I hadn't gotten a scholarship."

Julie was thunderstruck. What a lot of responsibility Nick was carrying around. She didn't know what to say. Fortunately, Brian and Bret called to Nick from a backseat, asking questions about the rodeo. By the time they pulled up at the K Bar K, Nick was in full flight, describing the various rodeo events. He didn't look at Julie again, concentrating on his discussion with the other kids, and Julie wondered if he was embarrassed that he'd opened up to her so much.

CHAPTER

NINE

All through lunch Julie was quiet, lost in her private thoughts. Nick usually ate with Bob and José, so she didn't see him again until it was time for the afternoon ride. And even then, he busied himself with the other kids' horses while Gary helped Julie get Maggie saddled.

Julie was annoyed, but there wasn't anything much she could do about it. Besides, she told herself, Nick probably has orders to make sure he gives everyone equal attention. Maybe he was just being overly careful that Gary saw him taking care of the others and didn't realize that Nick had a special interest in her.

In her mind's eye Julie saw herself and Nick riding through the valley and up into the hills together. Of course, while they were all still here at the K Bar K, the rest of them would have to be along. Even she could see that it wouldn't be fair for Nick to single her out and take her riding all alone. Unless the others had something else they'd rather do than ride . . . Julie shook the thought away. Let's not get totally ridiculous, she warned herself. There's no way he and I can spend time by ourselves as long as I'm staying here at the ranch.

Then a new idea struck her. What if she stayed on in Willow after next week when they were all supposed to go home? There was still plenty of summer left to get to know Nick better. Maybe she could get a job in town.

She'd done a lot of baby-sitting the last couple of years, and she was a good swimmer. If there was a local pool, perhaps they'd hire her to help out with the little kids. She could teach swimming, or if worse came to worst, she might be able to get a job as a waitress in one of the restaurants in town. And Martha had been so eager to get rid of her for two weeks that she'd no doubt send a little money if Julie would stay away longer.

Julie woke up from her daydream as Nick got on his horse and motioned for the rest of them to gather around. "It's about time for you to start thinking about the route you want to take on your solo ride next week," he told them. "You're all getting to be pretty good riders, so we'll split up into two groups this afternoon and take two different trails."

He glanced around at the kids. "Josh, you and Brian and Bret come with me, and the rest of you go with Bob and José." Then with a nod at Hannah, Roy, and Julie, he led his own little threesome off toward the woods.

Julie couldn't believe it. As she watched him ride away without even a backward glance, her mood darkened. How could he do this to her? Then she took a deep breath. Okay, fine with me, she thought angrily. Julie clucked to her horse, "Come on, Maggie, girl," and trotted after Bob, leaving Roy and Hannah to trail behind her, followed by José.

But once they were riding along, Julie's spurt of anger evaporated and she began to think about Nick in a more philosophical light. She'd already figured out that he was a little embarrassed because he'd told her so much about himself. That probably meant he rarely revealed his feelings to others, and that made their conversation special. She'd just have to find a way to let him know that it was okay to share your feelings with someone you liked. Sometimes guys were so dense, she thought. Nick probably didn't even realize that he and she were developing a special relationship.

But there was no chance to talk to Nick alone that afternoon. By the time they got back from their ride, dark clouds had drifted in over the mountains and everyone was in a hurry to get the horses taken care of before it started to rain. When she approached him in the barn, he looked uneasy and found an excuse to move off and help someone else, and before she knew it, he was getting ready to go home. Tears of frustration smarted in Julie's eyes as she watched him climb into his old pickup truck and start up the engine.

Julie tried to console herself with the thought that Nick might be worried about his mom and her house with the approaching storm. But she couldn't make the comforting idea take hold. She had to admit to herself that he was definitely avoiding her. And she didn't know what she could do about it.

During dinner the storm broke. Rain pelted down and thunder boomed along the valley. Through the big windows in the dining room they could all see the zigzags of lightning. The storm sounded ferocious.

For once Brian and Bret had a lot to say. They'd done a special section in school last year on the modern west and they were pleased that Nick had been able to fill them in on a lot of

rodeo details while they were riding with him
that afternoon.

The twins and Josh kept up an animated conversation about rodeos and rodeo riding and
what Nick had to say, while Julie sulked in
brooding silence. Great, she thought, they hang
out together doing guy talk and then they've got
the nerve to replay the whole thing now. I
should have been the one riding with Nick. They
could ask him a bunch of dumb questions some
other time.

The storm continued to rage outside and they
straggled into the living room after dinner.
There was nothing on TV; the storm had messed
up the reception from the ranch's satellite dish.
But there were quite a few movies on tape filed
neatly in a bookshelf next to the TV, and after
a heated discussion, they ended up voting on
which one they would watch.

Julie didn't care; she curled up in one of the
big easy chairs, and while her eyes were on the
TV screen, her mind replayed her conversation
with Nick in the van on the way back to the
ranch. Had she made a mistake encouraging
him to tell her so much about his life when
they'd hardly started their relationship? But no,
she decided, he'd been the one who'd shared all
that personal stuff about his mom and dad. She

hadn't done much more than be a good listener. Halfway through the movie the storm ended as suddenly as it had begun. Julie stretched and produced a big, fake yawn. "I'm going to read in my room," she announced, and then left.

A little while later Hannah came in. "That movie is about the dumbest thing I've ever seen. You were smart to leave when you did. It just got worse."

Julie was propped up on her bed with a book open on her lap. As it happened, she had hardly read a word, but there was no way Hannah could know that. Julie grunted a noncommittal comment and Hannah went into the bathroom.

Before long Hannah emerged with a bottle of skin lotion to begin her nightly routine. "You've been awfully quiet, Julie," the other girl said. "Is anything the matter?"

"No, of course not," Julie said, snapping her book shut. "Everything is just peachy keen." Her tone of bitter sarcasm reverberated in the room as she snatched up her nightshirt and stomped into the bathroom.

Back in the ranch-house living room the four boys were still watching the film. Josh looked at Roy, Brian, and Bret. All three of them were engrossed in the epic that would run another half hour at least.

Quietly Josh got out of his chair and gave a calculating look at the door leading to the rest of the house. It would be easy enough to slip through unnoticed. But who would he find on the other side? Too dangerous. There was no way he could explain what he was doing prowling around inside the house at night.

In fact he could hardly explain it to himself, except his instincts told him that something strange was going on here—something he wanted to find out more about. Finally he darted through the dining room and went outside, being careful not to let the screen door slam behind him.

Dark clouds still scuttled across the sky, blotting out the moon, and the ground was puddled and mushy. Josh crept along the outside of the house toward the bedroom wing. A window in one of the bedrooms had been raised a few inches to let in the fresh night air, and light streamed out through the partially opened shutters.

It must be Mrs. Fremont's room, Josh thought as he made his way toward it. The bushes growing along that side of the house had been clipped to below the edges of the windows and Josh figured he could see, or at least hear, what was going on in the lighted room. When he got up close, Gary's voice floated out.

"Don't give me any trouble," the man said. "I know what I'm doing."

"Sure you do." The woman's voice was sarcastic.

"We've done okay so far," Gary told her.

Josh edged nearer. He could see Gary pacing back and forth across Mrs. Fremont's bedroom, although he couldn't see the woman. It must be Mrs. Fremont, he thought. But her voice sounded so different from when she had been talking to the banker. Now it was much stronger.

"Look, I'm getting tired of all this playacting. Let's just get out of here," the woman pleaded.

"The only person going anywhere is Mrs. Fremont," Gary said. Then he smiled. "That bit about wanting to travel was plenty smart. Now we can just tell everyone she's gone away on a long trip. It's perfect. As soon as these kids leave . . ."

A figure rose from the bed. "Oh, Gary, I hate this whole thing," she wailed.

Gary reached out and pulled her close. "Now, now, Ilene. Everything's going to be fine."

Josh leaned toward the window, his mouth open in amazement. It was Gary's wife, Ilene, but she was wearing Mrs. Fremont's clothes!

As Josh stepped closer to the window to get a better look, he brushed against the bushes between him and the house. What seemed like buckets of cold water shook loose from the rain-soaked bushes, drenching the front of his shirt and splattering against the house. Josh sucked in his breath sharply.

Gary said, "What was that?" and yanked open the shutters.

Josh turned and ran. His thoughts tumbled wildly as he slipped and slid through the mud. What's going on here? Where did Mrs. Fremont go? He paused at the door to the dining room and then shook his head. He was soaked from the bushes and his shoes were covered with mud. Even the TV zombies would notice that he'd been outside if he slipped in now and tried to pretend he'd never left.

Instead he raced on to the entrance of the dormitory wing. Once inside, he walked noiselessly past Hannah and Julie's room. When he reached the large suite he shared with the other boys, he went in and closed the door quietly behind him. First thing he'd better do was get out of his wet clothes and wash the mud off his shoes.

Josh glanced over at Roy's bed as he headed toward the bathroom. A thought struck him.

This was the only time he was likely to be alone in the suite without one of the other guys coming in. The movie they were watching must have at least another fifteen minutes to run, maybe longer. And all three of them were totally absorbed in it. This might be his best opportunity to look through Roy's stuff and see if he could figure out what the other boy was up to. As soon as he got himself dried off and cleaned up, he'd get to it. And he'd better hurry.

CHAPTER

TEN

The next morning Julie felt a lot less cross than she had the night before. The whole outdoors had a fresh rainwashed smell and look. In Southern California, where it seemed rain was always in short supply, even the smallest amount caused terrible problems on the highways. But in spite of the traffic tangles and possible mud slides, Julie looked forward to rain because the first sunny day afterward was crystal clear and clean feeling. Her theory was that the rain beat the smog into the ground for a while. Of course, here the air was always clear, but today everything had a special brightness.

They saddled up right after breakfast and prepared for a sort of trial run for their solo ride at the end of the following week. Today would be a long ride, up to the summer hut for lunch and then back down to the barn, arriving at the ranch in time to change for an early dinner and then the rodeo in town. The main difference between today's ride and the one next week was that no one was going to be all alone.

"We'll use a buddy system," Nick told them. "I'll pair you up and then you decide between you what trail you want to take to the summer hut. But stay with your partner. It's still too soon for any of you to be wandering off by yourselves. Just remember that if you take off on your own, that means that your buddy will be left all alone."

As Nick watched them climb on their horses he seemed to be doing some sort of mental calculations. Then he said, "Okay, Julie, you go with Josh; Hannah, you're paired up with Roy; and Brian and Bret can go together." He grinned and went on, "Don't be surprised to have Bob or José or me join you at some point along the way. We'll be crisscrossing the area to check things out and make sure nobody has any problems. Then, after lunch, we'll all ride back down here together."

The kids moved off a little ways in their pairs and began low-voiced conversations while Nick conferred with Bob and José. Julie surreptitiously kept an eye on Nick. At least if she wasn't riding with him today, no one else would be either. Suddenly he looked over and caught her glance. He smiled and her heart lightened.

"Listen up," he called to them all. "You guys about set? Bob and José and I need to get the lunch stuff and take it up to the hut."

"Go ahead," Julie called back, and looked around to make sure everyone agreed. "We'll be fine. We're just figuring out which trails we want to take."

Nick nodded and, with one last quick look at the three pairs of teens on horseback, turned and led Bob and José toward the ranch house.

Julie returned her attention to Josh. "Which way do you want to go?" she asked. "It doesn't matter to me."

"You're certainly in an agreeable mood," Josh said.

Julie laughed. "Sure, why not? It's a gorgeous day and—" She stopped and watched as Josh deliberately dropped the key ring he'd been fiddling with and then laboriously got down off his horse to pick it up.

"What's with you?" Julie asked.

"Just keep talking," Josh told her. "Can't you see I'm stalling?"

"Why?"

Josh's voice came up to her in an urgent whisper. "I want to see where everyone else goes before we head out ourselves."

"For goodness' sake, Josh." Julie sounded exasperated. "Who cares what everyone else is doing? Why don't we get going and let them figure out a different trail from the one we're taking."

Josh clambered back up on his horse. "Look, you said you didn't care which trail we took?" He made it into a question and Julie nodded in agreement. "Well, neither do I. So we'll just hang out here for a couple of minutes pretending to decide and then we can see where the others go." He switched his gaze to Brian and Bret, who were heading out along the south trail. Then he turned back to Julie. "I told you I'm a detective. I need to know what's going on around me." He tried to make the explanation sound totally reasonable, but Julie knew better.

"You're just being nosy again," she said scornfully.

At that point Roy and Hannah moved off, Hannah taking the lead as they entered the narrow trail through the woods.

Julie watched Josh watching them. Then she said, "Okay, now can we go?"

"Sure," Josh told her. Then, indicating Roy's departing figure, he asked, "What do you know about him?"

"Who? Roy?" Julie shrugged. "Nothing. I

mean, what do we know about anybody here?"

"Well, doesn't he strike you as pretty weird?" Josh persisted. "He's always sneaking away to do something he doesn't want any of the rest of us to know about. So you gotta figure it's something strange. It might even be illegal."

Julie shook her head wearily. "Forget it, Josh. Has it ever occurred to you that maybe he just doesn't want to be around us?"

"That's not exactly true," Josh argued. "It's only when we're in town that he goes off like that." Then he snapped his fingers. "I got it. Maybe it isn't going *to* something, but away from it. Maybe it's the shelter that has him spooked—all those little kids." He spoke musingly. "And that might tie in with something I found in his drawer last night. It was a kid's book."

Julie's eyes widened in alarm. "Josh, you didn't!"

"Hey, a detective's got to take whatever opportunities present themselves," he said.

Julie sighed. "Look, can we just go? Everyone else has left."

Josh's face was clouded in thought for a moment, but then he grinned and nodded. "You know, I bet if we loop around the base of the mountain and go up the other side, we'll beat everyone to the summer hut," he said in an easy tone. "It sounds longer but I'm pretty sure it's actually faster."

Julie shrugged. "I didn't know it was a race, but fine with me."

They loped through the wide flat meadow that ran along the near side of the mountain. Both of them were much more secure on their horses than they had been at the beginning of the week, and now the riding was pure fun. Then they started up the steeper trail that led to the summer hut.

"You know, there's a lot of weird stuff going on around here," Josh told Julie once they were riding along side by side.

"Are you back on that Roy kick again?" Julie asked, her tone hostile.

"Not really," Josh told her. "There's other stuff, too."

Julie looked at him curiously. "Like what?"

"Like secrets I know." Now that he'd caught Julie's interest, he became coy. "I'm not ready to share them yet, even with you. I've got a few more things to figure out first. But maybe I'll leave you some clues."

"I'm not interested in poking into other people's business," Julie said flatly. "And I don't see why you are. You know, it's not the best way to make friends and influence people."

She gave Maggie a kick and trotted ahead of Josh, but he caught up and began talking again. "You know, Julie, it doesn't take a master detective like me to figure out you've got a major crush on Nick." He paused and grinned at her maliciously. "The question is, how does he feel about you? Maybe I should ask him."

"Don't you dare!"

"Now, now," Josh said mildly. "I'm only trying to help." By now Julie's face was beet red, but Josh wouldn't stop baiting her. "You want to be careful of that Pauline girl at the shelter, though. I don't know if you've noticed how she practically kisses the ground he walks on."

"Josh, give it a rest," Julie said between clenched teeth. "I'm warning you."

"Hey, Julie, I didn't know it was a sensitive issue with you," Josh said as if in surrender. "I just thought that if Nick wasn't aware of your feelings for him, I could sort of clue him in. You know, just man-to-man."

"You say anything, *anything* to Nick about me, and you're a dead person." Julie's voice was low and angry.

"Okay, okay," Josh said with an easy laugh. "Sometimes I think you're just a little bit touchy."

No wonder Roy always seemed ready to punch Josh out, Julie thought furiously. "Drop dead!" she snapped. Kicking Maggie into a gallop, she raced on up the hill and out of sight.

Josh grinned to himself and continued his deliberate pace up the wooded trail. But a few turns later he came upon Julie waiting for him. She told him stiffly, "Nick told us we had to stay together."

Josh gave her a mean grin. "Naturally. You couldn't very well tell him we had a fight, because he might ask what about. Besides, you certainly wouldn't want to be caught going against Nick's orders."

Julie glared at him and pressed her lips together as if to keep back the words she'd like to say. Then she turned and looked straight ahead, and the two of them rode the last few hundred yards to the summer hut without a word or glance between them.

But by dinnertime Julie had simmered down. It's stupid to let Josh's childish teasing get to me, she thought. She was chatting cheerfully to Hannah when Gary came in to give them instructions about the evening ahead. "Nick will take all of you in the van and park it in town near the street dance. You can walk from there to the rodeo and back."

He paused and looked at them sternly. "Everyone has to be back at the van by eleven-fifteen. Nick has orders to leave then, so if you don't get there in time, you'll have a very long walk back to the ranch. Any questions?"

"Are you going to the rodeo?" Josh asked.

"Of course, although not with you kids," Gary said. "This is one of the biggest events of the year. Everybody goes to the rodeo."

"So Mrs. Fremont's going too?" Josh had a sly expression on his face.

Gary looked at Josh for a moment. Then he said, "Well, no, Mrs. Fremont doesn't feel well enough to go. But she wants all of you to have a good time." He paused and then added, "She'll want to know that you all got back safe and sound. So don't disappoint her."

"Oh, we wouldn't want to disappoint Mrs. Fremont," Josh said, his voice sounding odd.

Now what's he up to? Julie asked herself. But the unspoken question was soon lost in the excitement of getting ready.

When they arrived in town, some of the streets were being barricaded for the dance and the rest were crowded with people.

"Where'd everyone come from?" Julie asked. "Willow doesn't seem like that large a town."

Nick grinned at her. "Oh, it isn't. But there are

a whole lot of ranches tucked away in the hills around here, and in the valley, too, of course. And this rodeo is really popular."

"No kidding," Julie said with a laugh. She liked standing close to Nick amid the bustling activity around them. It didn't take her long to imagine that the other kids in their group didn't exist, that she and Nick were going to the rodeo together. Almost like a date.

But Nick was doling out the tickets and explaining to the whole group how to get to the rodeo grounds. "It's plenty light now," he concluded, "but it will be dark when the rodeo lets out. So keep your eyes open on the way there and be sure you know where we're parked."

"Sounds easy enough," Josh commented. "But won't we all be together?"

Nick shook his head. "It's pretty hard to stay in a group, and besides we aren't all sitting in the same area." He smiled and went on, "Okay, get going. I'm stopping by the shelter on my way and see if anyone there feels up to a night in a crowd. I hustled up a few extra tickets, just in case." He gave them a grin that was clearly a dismissal. "I may be a little late getting there, but I don't want any of you to miss the beginning."

Almost before he'd finished talking, Hannah

snatched Julie's ticket out of her hand and
peered at it. "Are we sitting together? Oh, good,
we are. Come on, Julie, let's go."

Julie felt her unhappiness that Nick wasn't
walking with them evaporate as she and Hannah joined the enthusiastic crowd flowing toward the rodeo grounds. As they approached
the open gates in the chain-link fence, they
could see the ugly metal gridwork holding up
the bleachers. Right in front of them people in
temporary concession stands doled out cotton
candy and soft drinks. Julie thought in disappointment, It's just like a tacky local fair at
home.

But when she and Hannah circled the rear
curve of the bleachers and walked through the
narrow passage that opened onto the rodeo ring
itself, Julie gasped in astonishment. It was just
like a movie. No, it was better than a movie.
Across the huge dirt-floored ring were the
wooden gates of the animal chutes. And beyond
that, the mountains rose majestically, framing
the whole place like a painting of the Old West.
Over the hum of the crowd she could hear the
snorting of bulls and the whinnying of horses.
An announcer on the public-address system
welcomed everyone to the Willow rodeo and Julie could feel excited anticipation bubble up inside her.

"Come on, let's find our seats," Hannah said urgently. "It's about to start."

They showed their tickets to the cowboy standing at the entrance and then scurried across in front of the bleachers until they found their section. They reached their seats just as the national anthem began blasting from the loudspeakers.

When the last notes of "The Star-Spangled Banner" faded away, Julie sat down and looked around. They were almost in the center of the stands, near the front, where they had a perfect view of everything happening in the rodeo ring.

"And here she is, our own Willow rodeo queen, Samantha Hearn!" the announcer said excitedly. He rattled off the names of the queen's court as a blond girl rode out of one of the side gates and galloped around the ring. She was dressed in an all-red cowgirl outfit, including her boots and hat. And sequins glittered all over her shirt and pants. She was followed by three other young women also dressed in colorful western clothes, although not as flashy as the queen's. Dust billowed up from the horses' hooves as the four women circled the ring and waved at the fans in the bleachers.

"Her dry-cleaning bill must be enormous," Hannah whispered to Julie while the queen and her court stopped in front of the stands and bowed to the audience. Then they rode out of the ring and the announcer began calling out the first event.

Josh came trotting up the bleacher steps, looking for his seat, and squeezed in next to Hannah. "You missed the queen and her court," Julie said as everyone in their row moved over a bit to give him room.

"Who cares?" Josh replied. "I have more important stuff to take care of. Besides, I'm here for the good part." Suddenly he stopped speaking and watched openmouthed. The gate to the chute across the way burst open and a cowboy on horseback exploded out into the ring. The man was riding bareback, with only a strap around the horse's middle to hold on to, and his horse was bucking like crazy. "Look at that!" Josh said.

The horse careened all over the ring, bucking and twisting in spirals to dislodge the man on his back. The rodeo clown, perched on top of his metal safety barrel in the center of the ring, shouted encouragement to the cowboy to hold on, and two pickup cowboys kept their horses far away from the flying hooves.

In seconds it was over. The cowboy flew off the back of his bucking bronco and landed in the dirt while the horse dashed crazily around the ring. The pickup men and the clown hustled into action. While the men on horseback chased the frenzied animal to the far side of the ring, the clown raced over and helped the bronco rider get up and hobble out to safety. One of the cowboys reached across to undo a second strap around the bucking horse's middle, and relieved of both the strap and its rider, the animal settled down and trotted toward the open wooden gate.

"Isn't that amazing!" Julie said. "Now all of a sudden that horse acts like he's gentle as a lamb. Do they do something to make them buck like that?"

A man sitting behind them overheard her. "Don't let his gentle look fool you," he said. "Those bucking horses are born, not made. Sure, the other strap is annoying and makes him want to really buck it off. But you can't make a saddle-broke horse buck like that. All that horse needs is someone to try and climb on his back and he'll start bucking, strap or no strap. Rodeo contractors pay high prices for those natural buckers."

Before the man was finished talking, another bucking bronco and its bareback rider burst into the ring. This time the whistle blew before the horse bucked off its rider and the announcer called out the number of points the rider had made.

Everything happened so fast and there were no breaks in the action. After the bareback riding came calf roping, then saddle-bronco riding, followed by steer wrestling and team roping. Then the girls in the barrel race on their super-fast horses had everyone in the stands standing up and yelling encouragement.

Julie and Hannah had planned to run down to the concession stands and get sodas at some point, but Julie found she couldn't leave even for a few minutes. As soon as one event ended, another one started and her eyes were glued to the rodeo ring, trying to figure out what was going on. She leaned across Hannah and tried to talk Josh into going down to get them all drinks. But even her offer to pay didn't get him to budge. He, too, was enthralled with the rodeo.

"You planning on becoming a rodeo cowboy?" she asked him in a teasing tone, her earlier anger at him now almost entirely obliterated by the enjoyment of the moment.

Josh flashed her a quick grin. "You never know. Maybe I'm just watching to get a few pointers."

Then the first contestant in the bull-riding

event plunged out of the chute astride his huge, mean-looking bull, and Julie gasped. One of the cowboy's hands gripped the strap around the animal's middle, trying to hold on, while the other was held high in the air. The bull spun and bucked and twisted, fighting to throw off the man clinging to its back. When the bull did finally dislodge its rider, it turned, lowered its head, and charged.

The cowboy scrambled up as fast as he could and headed for the safety of the fence, but the bull was right behind him, obviously intent on doing as much damage as possible. Julie heard herself yelling, "No! No! Run!" Others were screaming, too, as if their voices could speed the cowboy out of harm's way.

The moment the cowboy flew off the bull and hit the ground, the rodeo clown and the pickup men on their horses started to move. The clown waved his arms and ran at the bull, trying to divert its attention from the fleeing cowboy. The men on horseback galloped around in an attempt to cut off the charging bull and corner it. But the bull, with its thousands of pounds of power and its wild, rolling eyes, seemed to see only one target.

Several men straddling the top of the tall white slatted wooden gate of the chute leaned down, their hands straining to reach the oncoming cowboy and pull him up to safety. The cowboy was nearing the gate, but the bull was closing in on him.

Then, just when it looked as though the cowboy was doomed, he reached the gate and scrambled up, the other men grabbing his arms and yanking him to the top. The bull charged into the gate, missing the cowboy's dangling feet by inches. The gate shimmied under the impact and a couple of the men were almost knocked off. But the gate held and this time everyone was safe. The crowd roared with approval and then quieted in anticipation of the next bull rider.

Julie sank back down onto the metal bleacher, her hand to her mouth. She realized that she'd been holding her breath and took a couple of big gulps of air. "I can't believe what I just saw," she said to Hannah. "That bull looked like he wanted to kill!"

"Oh, yeah," said the helpful man sitting behind her. "Some of those bulls are just plain mean. You take your bucking bronco, now he can be perfectly okay long as you don't try to ride him. But those bulls . . . I tell you, some of them would just as soon gore you or stomp you to death as look at you. Yes, ma'am, they're mean critters."

"But if it's so dangerous, why do people do it?" Julie asked him.

The man looked astonished. "Well, it's the sport."

"But they could get hurt!"

"Oh, sure, people do get hurt," the man assured her. "All the time. Didn't you notice that group of guys in wheelchairs down front when you came in?" Julie nodded and he went on. "Well, they always keep a flat section down in front of the bleachers so the crippled-up rodeo riders can see the show."

Julie's eyes got huge. "Oh, I see," she said, picking her words carefully. "Well, it's nice they have a spot where they can get a good view."

"Yup," the man agreed cheerfully. "You can't keep those old rodeo guys away. No matter what shape they're in."

Julie was saved from response by the announcement of the next bull rider and another eruption from the chute on the opposite side of the ring. This time the man stayed on the bull until the whistle blew, but he had trouble dismounting and getting to safety before the bull got to him. It's really exciting to watch, Julie thought, but I'm sure glad I'm not doing it.

She looked over at Josh. His pale face was stiff with tension. "Well, what now, cowboy?"

she asked. "Think you'll take up bull riding as your main event?"

Josh glanced back at her and Julie was surprised to see a flicker of fear in his eyes. But he answered in his usual jokey fashion. "Naw, I guess I'll leave that to the wimps. I'm made of sterner stuff," he told her.

Hannah laughed. "Sure, Josh. I'd love to see you on top of a mad bull."

Josh pulled himself up straight and addressed both Julie and Hannah in his most self-important tone. "In my business, it's brains, not brawn, that counts. I don't need to prove myself to anyone by getting banged around by a wild animal. Besides, I've got more important things on my mind."

Julie and Hannah dissolved in giggles, but underneath the laughter Julie felt some kind of formless dread. For a brief moment all her usual reactions to Josh—fondness, annoyance, and even occasional anger—were eclipsed by a feeling of overwhelming sadness. Then the emotion vanished and they were all laughing together.

The fireworks display at the end of the rodeo came as a wonderful surprise to Julie. No one had mentioned it before, and she loved watching the missiles and rockets bursting into colored flaring fragments while the loudspeakers played tinny patriotic music. The fireworks lit up the night sky and illuminated the outline of the mountains beyond the rodeo grounds. Everyone watched in awed silence, and when it was over the crowd began to move out.

Nick threaded his way through the bleachers, having a quick word with each of the kids from the K Bar K. When he got to Julie and Hannah, he asked, "You remember where the van is parked, right?" They both nodded and he went on. "Good. Just remember, be back there no later than eleven-fifteen. There's such a crowd that I won't be able to keep track of you, so keep an eye out for each other and I'll see you at the van."

He turned his gaze to Josh, who was standing on the other side of Hannah. "Did you get that?" he asked.

"Sure, no problem," Josh told him.

Nick looked over at a bunch of people leaving the stands and spotted Brian and Bret. "Okay. I gotta catch up to those two, but you guys take care. It might be a little wild in town tonight."

"Don't worry about us," Julie called after him. She turned to Hannah. "Well, are you ready for the street dance?" she asked with a grin. Then a look of confusion crossed her face. "Where's Josh? He was standing here just a second ago."

Hannah shrugged. "Don't know. He muttered something about seeing us later and then split."

Julie threw up her hands and then laughed. "Oh, well, we'll probably find out that he's wangled himself a job calling the square dance, or whatever they do. Let's go!"

The crowd was a little overwhelming, many bodies trying to get through the narrow gate of the rodeo grounds all at the same time. But there was no shoving or hostility; everyone seemed geared up for more fun ahead.

CHAPTER
ELEVEN

The back of the rodeo grounds, behind the chutes, was an eerie place to be late at night. A few work lights near the drive-through gate provided the only illumination and the animals in their pens were dark looming shadows.

In this part of the country, security didn't seem to be a big concern. Certainly the rodeo animals were valuable, but stealing any of them would definitely be a noisy and cumbersome business. So the livestock contractors had simply locked the drive-through gate and stationed a man in the nearby hut to make sure no one drove out with a bunch of horses. The owners themselves were probably off enjoying the festivities in town, feeling secure that their livestock had been fed and watered and bedded down for the night.

Josh had wandered back to the livestock area

after the rodeo and mingled with the cowboys and wranglers, waiting until the animals were settled. One by one and in small groups, the various workers left; Josh stayed out of sight until the last of them had gone.

It had been fun to watch the activity when there were lots of people around, but now the animals were his only company. The blanket of silence was broken by the sound of their large bodies shifting around, brushing up against the railings of their pens. From time to time he could hear the soft nicker of one of the horses or a snort from a bull.

How much longer would he have to wait? he wondered. The darkness was so intense he could barely make out the numbers on the illuminated face of his watch. Then he heard what he'd been waiting for.

"Psst. Over here." It was an unrecognizable voice, barely more than a harsh whisper, and it seemed to be coming from near the bullpen.

Warily Josh headed in that direction. "Where are you?" he whispered back. "I can't see a thing."

Josh listened intently, but all he could hear was a bull's heavy breathing as he approached its enclosure. The animal seemed to become more and more agitated as Josh got closer, perhaps sensing the boy's fear. Then he heard a step behind him. Before Josh could turn around, a heavy object crashed into the back of his head.

Julie and Hannah had had their fill of fun by the time the bank's brightly lighted clock read 11:04. They'd wandered through the streets of the small town, listened to the music, and even joined in the folk dancing for a while, but now they were tired.

As always seems to be the case in large, milling crowds, they kept recognizing the same strangers over and over again but rarely caught sight of anyone they knew. Earlier, when they first got to town, they'd seen Roy in earnest conversation with a pleasant-faced woman, but after that they hadn't seen him again. They'd spotted the twins from time to time, but they were never near enough to call hello. And they hadn't laid eyes on Josh even once.

Julie was hoping to see Nick, and she did. But he was always across the crowded street or in the middle of a group of local guys who all obviously knew one another and wouldn't have enjoyed some strange girl butting into their conversation. Then he, too, disappeared, and there was no one around she knew except Hannah.

For a while neither of the girls was willing to admit that they'd had enough, but finally Julie said, "Let's go back to the van. I'm beat."

"Fine with me," Hannah agreed. "It's been a long day."

Julie grinned at her. "You mean you don't always start out with an all-day ride and then go to a rodeo and wind up the evening with a street dance that spreads all over town?"

"Not usually," Hannah replied, laughing along with her friend.

They walked slowly along the sidewalk. When they were half a block from the van, Brian and Bret crossed the street and joined them. "Hi," Julie said. "Did you have fun?"

"Oh, yeah," Brian told her. "That rodeo was something else."

"Yeah, it was great," Bret added.

Julie tried to conjure up a mental picture of Brian and Bret separated all day on their solo rides next week. They were so constantly together that it was hard to imagine. It will be interesting to see how that works out, Julie thought.

When the four of them reached the van, they saw the back passenger door slid all the way open and Nick lounging against the hood of the vehicle. "Are we the last ones here?" Hannah asked.

"Nope," Nick said. "The first. But now that I've got four of you, there's only the other two to wait for. They'll probably be along anytime now."

They hung around for a few minutes, standing in a little group near Nick at the front of the van. No one had much to say. Julie felt too tired to be smiley and scintillating, and Nick hardly uttered a word. He looked grumpy and for once Julie saw things from what she perceived as his point of view.

What fun would it be for him to be shackled with a bunch of out-of-town teenagers on a Saturday night? He'd had just as hard a day as they had. Harder even, because he'd had the responsibility of watching out for all of them as well as the saddling and unsaddling of the horses, the stowing of gear, the setting up of lunch, and now driving them to and from town. Probably he would have liked to hang around with his pals. Maybe there were private parties that he'd been invited to. But he had his job, and now he was waiting silently, no doubt just wishing it would soon be over for today.

Julie sighed and wondered if Nick viewed her as a burden, or as just part of the larger burden of his job at the ranch. While she was immersed in these disquieting thoughts, Brian and Bret climbed into the van to wait.

Now eager to get going and be away from the uncommunicative Nick, Julie moved along the sidewalk, hoping to see the two remaining members of the group. Finally she spotted Roy walking rapidly toward them. But there was no sign of Josh.

"I'm not late," Roy said before he even got to the van. "It's exactly eleven-fifteen. Even by the bank's clock."

As Julie saw his defiant posture she thought, Roy certainly is a strange guy. One minute he's perfectly regular and the next he's defensive and prickly. Maybe Josh is right and there is something wrong with him.

Nick opened the driver's door. "Climb in," he said to Roy and Julie and Hannah, indicating the passenger door on the other side. "Let's go."

"But Josh isn't here yet," Julie protested. "We've got to wait for him."

Before Nick could say anything, Roy spoke up. "Let him be on time like everyone else if he wants a ride. Why should he be an exception?"

What a nerve! Julie thought. *He's* the one who's been an exception all along and we've been covering for him. She felt ready to explode. The simmering anger she'd felt all day, first at Nick and then at Josh, was now directed toward Roy. He was probably glad that Josh wasn't here yet, hoping that they'd leave the other boy stranded and make him walk home. Who knows, Roy could have even seen Josh talking to someone and not bothered to wait for him or tell the rest of the group that Josh was coming. If Roy knew that Josh had been run over by a car, he no doubt would have kept it to himself. That guy is such a weirdo, Julie thought angrily. Nothing he did would surprise me.

But before Julie could utter any of the indignant comments she had in mind, Hannah said to Nick, "Surely there's a grace period. I mean, Josh's watch may be slow or he might have stopped to talk to someone and not noticed the time. I can't imagine that he'll be long." Her tone was steady and reasonable, and Julie noticed that Hannah had cut Roy out of the discussion altogether.

"Hey, wait a minute. Rules are rules. I was hanging out with some cute girls, but I still left them to get back here when I was supposed to." Roy's voice was hostile and defiant. "I say let him walk."

"Well, Roy," Hannah said sweetly, "I like to think there's a little flexibility in all of us. I'm sure we'd all be willing to bend the rules a bit for you."

Roy flushed angrily but he didn't argue anymore. Instead, he went around to the other side
of the van and climbed noisily inside. Then he
moved to the far back corner and folded his
arms across his chest.

Nick's arms were folded across his chest, too,
as he leaned against the doorjamb on the driver's side. "Look," he said, "Gary was pretty serious about my leaving on time. He thinks it's a
matter of you guys acting responsibly. And he's
the boss."

"What about his responsibility to us, for our
safety?" Julie asked. "We can't just leave Josh
here in town and go on back to the ranch. What
if something happens to him?"

Nick looked at her steadily. "And what if he's
just messing around, figuring that we'll do just
what we're already doing and wait for him?" Julie glared at him and he lowered his gaze. Then,
after a moment he said, "Okay, we'll give him
another five minutes." He looked at Julie again.
"The worst that happens to him is that he hoofs
it all the way back to the ranch. But he'll probably snag a ride with someone. This is a small
town; it's not like he's in danger or something."

Julie drew Hannah aside while Nick stared
steadily down at his watch, seeming to count
off the minutes. "I can't believe that Josh would

just forget about the time," Julie told Hannah. "There must be some reason he hasn't showed up yet."

"Well, I hope it's a good one," Hannah said. "Nick's not looking too happy."

Julie couldn't explain to Hannah, or even to herself, exactly why she knew they shouldn't return to the ranch without Josh. But the feeling was too strong to be denied. "Hannah, we can't let the van leave without him. I just don't feel right about it. We've got to find a way to stop Nick if he decides he's really going to go."

Hannah gave Julie a quizzical look. "What did you have in mind? Throwing ourselves in front of the wheels?"

Julie didn't bother to laugh. "Maybe we could fan out in a search party and look for him."

"Oh, sure. Nick's going to love that idea. Now that he's got five of us rounded up, he's going to cut us loose to go looking all over town. For all he knows, none of us would come back."

Julie frowned. She could see that Hannah had a point, and really there was no reason for her own worry. But she couldn't stop herself. She marched up to the open passenger door of the van and called inside. "Did any of you guys see Josh after the rodeo?"

Brian said, "He was still standing in the

bleachers with you and Hannah when we were leaving."

"Yeah, we didn't see him at all after that," Bret told her.

"What about you, Roy?" Julie insisted, even though Roy was pretending to be asleep. "Where did you see Josh last?"

"I don't know," Roy said, his voice drowsy and disinterested. Julie waited, tapping her finger on the van door, and eventually Roy opened his eyes and glared at her. "Look, I was doing my own thing. It wasn't my job to keep an eye on Josh. But I didn't see him at all after the rodeo let out."

Julie walked around to the other side of the van and faced Nick. "Hannah and I aren't getting in the van. So if you decide to go without Josh, you're going to have to leave us here, too." Nick sighed when he heard the determination in her voice. "No one's seen Josh in town at all tonight, unless you have?" She made it a question and Nick shook his head. "Well, then I think we'd better look for him. Or maybe call the police."

Nick pulled himself upright and nodded glumly. "I'll use the pay phone on the corner and call Gary," he said. "The rest of you stay put right here till I get back."

It was well after midnight before the search

for Josh began in earnest. Gary arrived in town
where the van was parked soon after Nick's call.
He told them all that he'd gone home early because Ilene felt she was coming down with
some bug and wanted to get into bed. The sheriff and his two deputies questioned Nick and the
kids again to see if anyone had an idea of where
Josh could be. But, according to everyone, the
last time he'd been seen was when he was
standing beside Hannah in the stands at the conclusion of the rodeo.

"You better get these kids back to the ranch,"
Gary told Nick when the sheriff had finished
questioning them and had gone to organize his
deputies.

"No!" Julie protested. "We want to stay here
and find out what's happened to Josh." She
didn't know for sure that the rest of them agreed
with her, but she didn't care.

"It's already late and who knows how long
they'll need to look," Gary said, trying to convince them. But his words were greeted with
stony resistance. "Look, maybe Josh has already gone back to the ranch. He could have
hitched a ride and we could have passed each
other on the road."

"No way," Julie said defiantly. "We were right
here with the van the whole time. If he'd just

been late, he would have found us—he'd be
here now." Then another thought struck her. "If
you really think there's a possibility he's at the
ranch, you'd better call there and have Ilene
check. You wouldn't want the sheriff and his
men to be wasting their time."

Recognizing defeat, Gary grumbled something to Nick about keeping all of them inside
the van until he came back. Then he went to
join the sheriff in the search.

By this time the street dancing had long since
stopped and most of the townspeople had gone
home. The deputies walked the empty streets,
shining their flashlights behind Dumpsters in al-
leys and into the doorways of darkened shops.
They checked inside the hotel and the bars that
were still open. Then they walked back along
the road to the rodeo grounds, searching the
bushes and the ditch as they went.

Gary and the sheriff met them at the rodeo
grounds and together they looked underneath
the bleachers, in the seating area itself, and
through all the little outbuildings. When they got
to the hut where the livestock security guard sat
dozing, he told them that one of the bulls had
been raising quite a fuss a couple of hours earlier, but had quieted down soon after.

Finally they shone their lights on the livestock enclosures. There they found Josh, crum-
pled in the corner of one of the bullpens.

CHAPTER

TWELVE

They heard the siren before they saw the ambulance. It went screaming past the minivan and disappeared in the direction of the rodeo grounds.

Turning back again in her seat in the van, Julie caught the nervous expressions on the twins' faces. Roy's eyes were closed, but his hands were tightly clenched fists in his lap.

She looked at Hannah. The other girl was staring at her, her eyes full of questioning concern. Julie stared back. Was the ambulance for Josh? She felt with cold certainty that it was, and she guessed Hannah must think so, too. But she was grateful that the other girl hadn't put the question into words. Saying it aloud would make it true. A superstitious shiver of dread trickled down Julie's spine.

They sat there in silence, until at last the Jeep

pulled up next to them. Gary got out and walked heavily to the open door of the van. He looked at each of them in turn and they stared back. "I have bad news," he said. Julie's blood pounded in her ears and she found herself unable to breathe as he continued, "We found Josh. He was in one of the bullpens at the rodeo grounds—he's hurt pretty bad."

"Is he dead?" Julie hardly recognized her own voice.

Gary shook his head. "No, but . . . he's unconscious, and they won't know how bad it is until they get him to the hospital."

"Let's go, then—we should be there with him." Julie looked at Nick in urgent appeal.

Gary shook his head. "No, there's nothing you can do, and you'll just be in the way. Nick will take you back to the ranch—I'm staying here."

Julie could see that arguing would get her nowhere, but she extracted a promise from Gary that he'd let them know the minute there was any change in Josh's condition.

It was a mournful little group that made its way back to the ranch in the van. Nick and the boys said nothing, while tears filled Hannah's eyes and Julie sat silently weeping.

When Julie and Hannah entered their room, clutching the mugs of hot chocolate that Ilene had supplied, Julie said, "I just don't believe it."

Hannah sat down slowly on the edge of her bed. "I know. It doesn't seem possible. One minute he was right there with us, wisecracking like always, and the next . . ." She put her hands to her face. "It's too awful to think about. How could he have done something so stupid as to climb into that bull's pen?"

Julie blew her nose and wiped the tears off her face, but new ones replaced them. "That's the part I don't understand. Why would Josh do such a thing?"

They turned out their lights, but Julie lay sleepless for a long time. How had Josh gotten into the bullpen? He'd been afraid of the bulls, even from the safety of the bleachers. Pictures of Josh's smart-aleck smile and carrot-red hair pushed into her mind, and she heard his teasing voice telling her he'd learned some secrets. She stifled a sob. Was Josh going to be okay?

The next morning Gary told the subdued group at breakfast that Josh was still unconscious. He'd tried to get in touch with Josh's parents, but they were off on a mountaineering trek in Nepal and it wasn't clear how soon they would get his message.

"Can we go and see him?" It wasn't that Julie didn't believe Gary, but she wanted to see Josh

for herself. How could he still be unconscious?
Had the bull kicked him in the head? Maybe the
presence of his friends would help him wake up.

"Not now," Gary told her. "The doctor doesn't
want him to have visitors. Maybe later—we'll
have to wait and see." He looked at the somber
faces around the table. "I know this is tough for
you all to deal with, but I think maybe the best
medicine is to get on with things here at the
ranch. Nick will be over a little later and you
can all go for a ride. Being out on the land is
often very healing."

He was turning to leave when he remembered
something else he needed to say. "Mrs. Fremont
isn't feeling well, so she can't come in this morning in person. But she asked me to tell you all
how terribly sorry she is. She knows that Josh's
accident has affected you deeply, but she hopes
you'll be able to enjoy the rest of your time
here."

When Gary left, the other kids began to talk
in low voices, but Julie sat immobile, unable to
put her thoughts together coherently. When
Hannah spoke to her, she could hardly grasp the
words. "I'm sorry," she blurted, "I've just got to
be by myself." And she raced out of the dining
room. Hannah started to follow her and then
thought better of it. Maybe Julie did need to be
alone for a while.

Julie wandered aimlessly along the stream, taking in deep breaths of the clean cool morning air and trying to make sense of what had happened. Eventually she found herself heading for the dorm end of the ranch house. The others were still at breakfast and the bedrooms were empty.

She went into the boys' room and sat down on Josh's bed. Absentmindedly, she fingered through the jumble of stuff on his bedside table. There was that dumb key ring he sometimes carried around. He'd told her once that the midget magnifying glass attached to it was to help him find clues, but the plastic lens was so scratched up that it was impossible to see through. Then she noticed that he'd brought some books with him. All of them were spy novels. Julie smiled sadly as she imagined how Josh probably saw himself as the hero in every one of them. What clues could he have thought he'd find in that bull's pen?

Julie picked up the books and held them in her lap. Maybe it was just some dumb stunt, sitting on top of the pen enclosure to prove he wasn't afraid. Then the bull had rammed the fence, knocked him inside, and trampled him.

Tears dripped from Julie's face onto the books and she reached for a tissue to wipe them off. Under the box of tissues, shoved to the back of the nightstand, was a little notebook with a pen stuck inside its spiral binding.

As Julie opened it and began to read, she realized it was some sort of diary. More precisely it appeared to be the information he said he was always gathering about the people around him. Julie gave a little choked laugh. He probably thought of it as his detective notebook. Sure enough, on the inside of the front cover he had written *Josh Malone, Ace Detective.*

Unfortunately Josh's handwriting was messy and hard to read. And he'd used some sort of code so that Julie felt she was guessing about the content of the first few pages.

Suddenly the door to the room opened and Gary walked in. He was just as surprised to see Julie as she was to see him. "What are you doing in here?" he demanded. Then he must have realized how harsh the question sounded because he continued in a softer tone. "I thought you were still at breakfast with the others."

Quickly Julie shut the notebook. "Oh, I guess I was just thinking about Josh," she said in confusion.

Gary gave her a sympathetic smile. "I know you're upset about what happened. But really, the best thing is to try to get back to some sort of normal routine." He looked around the bed she was sitting on. "I'm going to pack up Josh's stuff—he probably won't be able to come back to the ranch."

He walked to the end of the bed and reached under it, looking for Josh's duffel bag. While his back was turned Julie slid the notebook off her lap and put it down beside her on the bed. For some reason she didn't want Gary handling Josh's private notebook. Carefully she tried to move the books off her lap and onto the bed to cover up the diary. Then maybe he wouldn't even notice it and would bundle it up with the rest of Josh's stuff.

Gary straightened abruptly, the fugitive duffel bag under his arm. His eyes fastened on Julie's hands sliding Josh's other books over to hide the spiral notebook. He walked back around the bed and stood in front of Julie, staring down at her. "What's that?" he asked, indicating the notebook. "Something of Josh's?"

Julie looked up at him with guilty eyes. Probably it had been an invasion of Josh's privacy for her to start reading his secret notes, but she hadn't thought of it that way until now. She nodded and said, "It's kind of like a diary."

Gary snatched up the notebook and held it, glaring at Julie. "How much of this did you read?"

"I only barely opened it," Julie told him miserably.

Gary continued to look at her skeptically and Julie dropped her eyes. Finally he said, "Well, I've got to get these things packed up and out of here. So I suggest you go back to the dining room." He stuck the notebook in his pocket and then began pulling clothes out of one of the bureau drawers.

As Julie left the room she didn't see Gary turn and watch her go. The look on his face was not pleasant.

Nick had their horses in the corral and was getting ready to saddle them up for the ride. Brian and Bret were helping him while Roy stood feeding his horse a sugar lump and stroking his nose.

Hannah came up to Julie and linked her arm in the other girl's. "They're packing a picnic and taking it down to the river, so we'll ride for a while and then go over there," she said. "We should take our suits," she went on, trying to sound enthusiastic. "Nick says there's a place we can probably go swimming."

"Why don't you guys go on without me," Julie said in a tired voice. "I'm really not in the mood for a picnic."

"Come on, Julie," Hannah urged. "I know

you're upset; we all are. But that's not going to help Josh." Hannah gave her a gentle push. "Please," she added.

Nick had obviously given some thought to the mood of the group when he chose the route for their ride. They went across gently rolling hills along the base of the mountains, and the open fields allowed room for them to spread out in a loose formation. While in sight of one another, no one was actually riding with anyone else. There was no need, in fact no opportunity, for conversation. And the terrain was right for easy riding. Sometimes they ran their horses, at others they walked at a leisurely pace, but there was never much need to concentrate on what they were doing.

Julie let her thoughts wander. At first all she saw was the brutal comparison between the relentless beauty of the countryside and Josh lying unconscious in a hospital bed. She wondered whether his parents had even heard yet about his accident. How would they feel, so far away from their son? And that led to thoughts of her own family at home. She realized with amazement that somewhere along the line she'd let go of the hot anger she'd felt toward her stepmother.

Oh, she and Martha were unlikely to end up

as best friends, but somehow being away from
home had put things in a different perspective.
Maybe Martha's motives weren't entirely self-
serving. It couldn't be much fun living in a house
with a teenager who hated you and a husband
who was caught in the middle. Yet Martha had
continued to be cheerful and friendly and had
never given Julie anywhere near the amount of
misery that Julie had handed out.

Maybe things can be a little better between
us when I get home, Julie thought. And then Dad
won't have that worried look he always gets.
She knew that the constant tension in the house
was the source of her father's anxiety, and that
she was the source of the tension. Her dad so
much wanted her and Martha to get along. Well,
I can give it a try, she decided.

Instead of going on the ride, Bob and José had
spent the time lugging an enormous picnic
down to the river. They'd set up portable tables
for the food and had a pile of blankets ready to
spread on the ground.

Julie purposely dawdled and was the last to
arrive. She dismounted and led Maggie down to
the river for a drink and then tied her to one of
the low trees near the other horses. José and
Bob had also brought along a tin of oats, so Julie
scooped up a handful and offered them to Mag-

gie. The horse nickered its appreciation and its gentle lips brushed Julie's fingers. Julie threw her arms around the glossy brown neck. "You don't say much, but I bet you understand everything, don't you, girl," Julie whispered.

The sight of the bountiful spread on the table reminded Julie of how hungry she was—she hadn't eaten much breakfast. Filling her plate with food, she spread a blanket on the grassy bank of the river. With the exception of Nick and Bob and José, who were busy organizing the meal, everyone else did the same.

They were a quiet group, but they all managed to eat a lot. After they'd finished, Nick and Bob took care of cleaning up while José got out his guitar and began to strum it in a gentle, slow rhythm. Julie felt her eyelids drooping. The combination of his soft voice and the steady ripple of the river was so soothing to listen to. She stretched out on her blanket, propping her head against a convenient rock, and in moments she was fast asleep.

In her dream she was riding Maggie, loping through the tall summer grass. Josh was riding his horse, too, in the same field. He kept calling to her, but she couldn't catch his words. It seemed that what he wanted to tell her was important, but no matter how hard she tried, she couldn't steer Maggie any closer to him. She strained to hear what he was saying, but the only sound she heard was that of the rushing wind.

Then, suddenly, Josh veered away and disappeared from view. She scanned the horizon, but there was no sign of him. Maybe he'd gone back to the ranch. She wheeled Maggie around and then somehow they were headed down a steep slope. The smooth grasslands had changed into a treacherous, rocky terrain. Maggie stumbled and it was all Julie could do to hang on. But the horse got her footing again and raced forward.

Faster and faster they flew down the slope, Julie pulling back on the reins to no avail. She could hear her heart thumping in fear. It sounded like the pounding of a horse's hooves. Then the sound stopped.

"Looks like siesta time," a voice said, and Julie's eyes popped open. Gary was just getting down off his horse. "Are you here all by yourself?" he asked her.

Startled out of a deep sleep, Julie looked around wildly. The picnic food had all been stashed away in the coolers, the tables taken down, and all the blankets but hers neatly folded in a nearby pile. The others were nowhere to be seen. She and Gary were alone.

"Uh, uh," Julie stammered. "I guess I fell asleep."

"I guess you did," Gary agreed. He ambled down to the water's edge and gazed up and down the river. "Looks like they left and went off exploring without you," he said, still facing the river. "I can't see them anywhere."

Gary turned and walked toward where Julie sat, his gait steady and purposeful. The sun was at his back and all Julie could see was the silhouette of a large male figure getting nearer. She scrambled to her feet. Something about being alone with him made her nervous. Quickly she picked up the edge of her blanket and shook the whole thing hard. Gary put his arm to his face to protect his eyes from the flying dust and grass bits. "Hey, watch it," he told her, his voice sharp and angry.

"Oh, sorry," Julie mumbled. Then she slapped the blanket together in a somewhat folded heap and backed up to drop it on top of the others. "Well, I guess I'd better get along and find everyone else," she said in a bright, brittle voice. "They're probably wondering what's happened to me."

As Julie edged toward where Maggie was still tied, Gary moved to catch up with her. "But you don't know where they've gone," he said, his voice silky. "I think you should wait here for them to come back."

Julie felt the presence of her horse close behind her. She reached out and loosened the reins from the tree limb. "No, I don't want to." Even to her own ears, she sounded like a petulant child refusing to do the logical thing. But, idiotic as it was, she felt almost afraid to be here with him any longer.

Gary's hand snaked out and grabbed her arm. "I want you to stay," he told her. There was something menacing about the way he said it and she trembled in his grasp.

For a moment Julie considered yanking her arm away. Could she jump on her horse and be out of there before he could get on his own and follow her? And where would she go? She felt his fingers tighten around her wrist.

Before Julie could decide what to do, her eyes caught sight of the corner of Josh's diary sticking up from Gary's shirt pocket where he'd put it earlier. "You still have Josh's notebook," she blurted out accusingly.

Gary's other hand reached up and patted his shirt pocket. "Yes, I guess I do," he said with an odd smile. "Why don't you come back and sit down and we can talk about that?"

"Hey, Julie!" It was Hannah calling to her from the middle of the river. She was crossing on horseback and Julie could see Nick not far behind her. "Come on! We found this great swimming hole."

Julie sighed with relief as Gary dropped her wrist and stepped back. "Well, I guess we'll have that discussion some other time," he said. "You've got your pals to play with." He turned and waved at Hannah and Nick and then walked over to his horse.

After he climbed into his saddle, he swept his arm in an arc, shooing her toward the river and Hannah. "Run along, now," he said. "Go with your friends." Then he added softly, "Just remember, I'll be keeping an eye on you, Julie."

Julie quickly clambered up on Maggie's back and bolted toward the river while Gary rode off in the other direction. As she joined Hannah and Nick, who turned around to recross the water, she wondered what was the matter with her. Surely Gary had just been being overly protective. Probably after what happened to Josh, he was feeling nervous about other possible accidents and was acting extra-cautious. But another part of her brain refused to accept that innocent explanation for the way he'd behaved.

It was crazy to think that Gary was actually

dangerous. Julie wasn't going to let herself get sucked into that kind of paranoia. She realized that she was exhausted and emotionally drained, not the best way to be when you wanted to think clearly. Still, there was something peculiar in the way Gary had been acting. He'd had a kind of determined insistence on their being alone together, sort of like the way some guys at school behaved when they were gearing themselves up to ask her out. Ugh, she thought. That couldn't be what Gary had in mind. It was too disgusting to contemplate.

Later, when the two of them were sitting in the grass next to the swimming hole, Julie asked Hannah, "What do you think of Gary?"

Hannah didn't respond immediately, obviously mulling over her answer. Finally she said, "I don't have any opinion about him at all. He's just the guy who runs the ranch."

Cautiously Julie looked around to make sure no one was near enough to hear her. Even though they were alone, she leaned a little closer to Hannah. "Then what would you say if I told you I think maybe he was coming on to me back there?" she asked.

"Gary?" Hannah looked at Julie in disbelief. "Please. Give me a break. He doesn't look like a guy who'd know how to come on to anyone."

She wrinkled her nose in distaste. Then she asked, "What happened?"

By the time Julie finished her recital of the events back at the picnic spot, she didn't know what to think herself. Everything sounded so innocent. He hadn't actually done or said anything that she could point to in support of her statement.

"Let's get real here, Julie," Hannah told her. "The guy startled you out of a sound sleep, and when you got all nervous and decided to take off on your horse by yourself, he tried to stop you. That doesn't sound very sinister." She looked thoughtful for a moment and then went on. "Still, if that's how he made you feel . . ."

Her voice trailed off and Julie said quickly, "It isn't exactly how I felt, but it's the only thing that makes some kind of sense. All I know is that he was weird." She paused. "Funny, that's what Josh always said, that there was a lot of weird stuff going on here."

Hannah stretched her arms and wriggled her toes. "Well, I'd just make sure I didn't spend any time alone with Gary if I were you. Whatever his problem is, it doesn't have to be yours, too. Come on, I want to get wet again."

CHAPTER

THIRTEEN

The next morning Julie and Hannah walked out to the minivan after breakfast. They'd asked again if they could visit Josh, and although Gary said the doctors didn't want them in the intensive-care room, they could go to the hospital on their way back to the ranch, and at least look at him through the window. Julie was looking forward to it. It was better than nothing, and she realized that somehow she needed to actually see Josh with her own eyes.

Roy was already sitting in the front passenger seat, next to where Nick would be in a few moments. Julie would have liked to sit there herself, and she was tempted to ask Roy to move. But a quick glance at Roy's hostile expression changed her mind, and Julie climbed into one of the minivan's backseats next to Hannah. As the twins came rushing up to join them, Julie wondered again at Roy's prickly attitude. Sometimes she thought he had a perpetual chip on his shoulder. And Josh had been like a magnet for Roy's anger. They had managed to clash on almost everything.

Then she remembered Roy's enthusiasm for the playground project at the shelter and his occasional willingness to help. It was as if he was agreeable to working so long as he could get his time alone in town as well. What was he doing when he was away from the shelter? she wondered, not for the first time. But she pushed the question firmly aside. She had other things to think about.

Julie had tried to put her encounter with Gary out of her mind. She'd already spent enough time the night before rerunning the whole thing. By the time she fell asleep, she wasn't sure at all that Gary had been coming on to her, but she couldn't imagine what else he could have been up to. There was something definitely odd about the incident and it had left her feeling nervous and wary.

They arrived at the shelter and discovered that Etta's contact for the tractor tire had already delivered what he'd promised. The gigantic tire lay in the alley outside the playground, near the padlocked gate. "It was some man named Ralph Wiggs," Pauline told them as she led them down the alley to look at it. "He said Nick's mom asked him to bring it over and leave it here."

There was a questioning look in the girl's eyes, and Julie realized that Pauline and the others must not know about the playground plans. She glanced across at Nick. Why hadn't he already told them? Did he want to keep it as a surprise? Or was he worried that the kids from the ranch would forget all about their plans for the shelter in the wake of Josh's accident?

Nick's face remained impassive. Clearly it was up to Julie and the others to decide now if they were going on with this major undertaking. They still had time to back out and just tell Pauline that the tractor-tire delivery had been a mistake.

After a quick look at the others to confirm what she already knew, Julie plunged right in and told Pauline about their ideas for a playground. "It's not going to be perfect," she ended up. "We've got less than a week. But we'll do the best we can."

Pauline grinned. "Anything you do will be better than what we've got now," she told them. Then she paused and her face reflected genuine sadness. "I'm really sorry about your friend

Josh. That was a terrible thing to happen."

Julie nodded soberly. "Thanks, Pauline. We're hoping he's going to be okay. But without him to help, we may not get as much done as we'd planned."

"Well, golly, there's no reason I can't help you." Pauline blurted out the words and then seemed a little nervous about making the offer. "I mean, if you don't mind. I wouldn't want you to think I'm butting in on your project."

Julie was surprised. She had never given any thought to how the women at the shelter would view the little band from the ranch. She'd just assumed they'd be grateful. That would make everybody happy. The people at the shelter would have stuff they really needed, and Julie and her friends could feel good about what they'd done. She hadn't really understood that Pauline and the others might get a little tired of being grateful to people who loaded them up with hand-me-downs and other stuff because they felt sorry for them.

"Hey, Pauline, we'd be thrilled if you could help," Hannah said quickly. "After all, it's your project, not ours. We're just getting this started. It'll be up to you guys to make it work and keep it going."

As they walked back to the school's front entrance, Julie thought, Hannah is so quick on the uptake. She always seems to understand things before I do.

Once again the shelter was prepared for their arrival. All the kids were gathered in one of the rooms, and Julie could hear the soft murmur of a woman reading to them as she passed the closed door. She and the others started setting up the equipment for painting while Pauline and Nick searched for the key to the playground gate's padlock. Then they all went outside to roll in the huge tire and supervise its placement in the playground.

While they were out there a truck from the feed store pulled up and dropped off the mulch and other stuff for the garden. Hannah stayed out back with the twins and Roy to plot out the garden and start digging up the hard, dry soil while Nick went inside to the playroom with Julie and Pauline. Julie suspected that Roy would somehow be missing from that group outside before long, and she wondered again what he wanted to do in town that was so important.

After Nick instructed Julie and Pauline on the fine points of painting the shelves, he left to go out and work on the garden. Julie watched the other girl's face as Nick ambled out. "I guess

Nick has been a big help to you guys," Julie said when he was out of earshot.

Pauline sighed happily. "Oh, yes. And Nick is such a decent person." She laughed ruefully. "Unlike other guys I could mention."

Julie felt a spurt of jealousy. She guessed that Pauline had seen a lot of Nick before Julie arrived at the ranch, and she'd have that time alone with him again if Julie left when she was supposed to. Still, she had been curious all along about what had brought Pauline to the shelter, and now was her opportunity to find out. She hesitated, not knowing exactly how to start.

Then Pauline solved the problem for her. "Derek was his name, in case you're wondering."

"Your husband?" Julie asked.

Pauline shook her head. "No, we were just living together. We'd been going together my last year of high school, but my folks thought he was too old for me. So as soon as I graduated, Derek and I moved to Bozeman. He had a job with a trucking company and we got a cute little apartment. It was so romantic. At least at first. Then I began to see a side of him I'd never known existed before. He hung out late at night with his buddies drinking."

Terrific, Julie thought, a truck driver who

drinks. That's really great.

Pauline stared down at her hands as she went on. "It wasn't so bad at the beginning. He just yelled at me, saying the apartment was a pigsty and he knew I was running around on him and stuff like that." She looked squarely at Julie. "That wasn't true, none of it."

She seemed to be waiting for some sort of response, so Julie said, "Oh, guys can say a lot of rotten things they don't mean when they drink." Although Julie knew nothing about this except what she had picked up from TV, it seemed to satisfy Pauline.

"Right, that's what I thought. That he didn't mean it. And I thought the same thing when he started slapping me. He always apologized the next day." Pauline was staring down at her hands again. "But finally, well, things escalated, and I had to get out of there."

"Why didn't you go home to your parents?" Julie asked.

Pauline shrugged. "I guess I was too embarrassed. All I would have gotten was a lot of 'I told you so.' Besides, Derek knows where my folks live. I was sure he'd track me down there; he'd said he'd kill me if I tried to leave him." Her voice had dropped to a whisper. "Then I heard about this place, so here I am."

How horrible, Julie thought, to be afraid of someone you'd loved. "Did Derek come here looking for you?"

"Oh, yeah. I found out he was in Willow asking around about me. But no one on this side of the mountain knows me, except Nick and the people here at the shelter." She gave Julie a wry grin. "So he went away empty-handed. And so far he hasn't come back."

Julie was stunned into shocked silence. How would she have coped with something like Pauline had been through? She wasn't sure she would have been able to handle things as well as the other girl seemed to be doing. Finally she asked, "What are you going to do now? I mean, you can't just stay here forever, can you?"

Pauline shook her head. "Oh, no. This isn't a permanent place to live, just a temporary shelter till you get your life back on track again." She dipped her brush into the paint and carefully laid an even coat on one of the shelves. "I've given it a lot of thought. I figure I'll try to get a waitress job in town or even work as a maid at the hotel. Eventually I could save enough to get my own apartment. That's what some of the other women here are doing, and I don't have kids to worry about like they do."

Julie thought that at least that was one thing

Pauline had to be thankful for. Pauline had gotten out of high school just over a year ago and it sounded as though she didn't have any job skills. How would she have supported herself and a child? How could she have made a life for a little kid when she hadn't even had much of a life herself so far?

The two girls painted in silence for a few minutes. Julie wanted to say something comforting, something uplifting. But she didn't have a clue as to what that might be.

Then Pauline said wistfully, "Nick thinks I should go to college in the fall. The place he goes has work programs, so you can earn almost enough to get by. And I got really good grades in high school, so maybe I could get some kind of scholarship or loan." She looked at Julie and grinned. "Nick says that if I'm going to wait tables or work as a maid, I might as well get a college education at the same time."

"I think that's a wonderful idea!" Julie said. "Have you applied?"

Pauline shook her head. "No. It's probably already too late. And besides, I'd be a whole year older than everyone else in my class. And, no matter what Nick says, I don't think there's any way I could earn enough money to make it."

Julie knew enough about applying to college

to realize that the summer before you wanted to start was awfully late to apply. But maybe there were exceptions for special circumstances. "I don't believe Nick would have encouraged you to try unless he thought there was a good chance you could get in. There could be some kind of special program that he knows about and you don't. As for being a year older, there are grandmothers who go to college. I see these people all the time on TV. One year wouldn't make any difference at all."

Pauline was still shaking her head. "I don't think it would work. My folks aren't about to give me any money. They'd just say I'd made my bed and now I have to lie in it."

Julie was exasperated. Pauline kept throwing up roadblocks even though Julie could tell that the other girl really wanted to go back to school. "Well, maybe there's a way for you to earn some money this summer. You've got at least six weeks till college starts." Then Julie got an inspiration. "Have you met Nick's mom? She's really terrific and I'll bet she could come up with some ideas."

Pauline looked steadily at Julie. "I only see Nick when he's here. I've hardly been out of this place since I came."

"Well, think about it, Pauline," Julie told her.

"You've got to try every way you can figure out how to help yourself when you're in a tough spot."

"Yeah, you'd know a lot about that," Pauline said, blinking back the angry tears forming at the corners of her eyes. She put down her paintbrush. "I think I'll see if they need my help outside." She got up from where she was crouched by the shelves and left.

Julie watched Pauline's stiff back as she went out the door. Nice going, she told herself sarcastically. You and your big mouth and all your great advice. She dipped her brush in the paint and savagely applied it to the wood. "What an insensitive clod you are, Julie Stone," she muttered aloud to the empty room.

CHAPTER

FOURTEEN

On the way back to the ranch Julie thought again how much she missed Josh. It had been a relief to see him at the hospital, but it had also been pretty scary—he was just lying there with his eyes closed, hooked up to a bunch of machines. Only the little green blips on the screen across the room showed that he was alive. The times she'd been angry with him were now pretty much forgotten, and she wished he were there in the minivan joking around like before. When the rest of them trooped into the dining room for lunch, Julie told Hannah that she'd be along soon. Then she went into the boys' room for another look at Josh's corner.

Of course she knew his stuff would be gone, packed up by Gary. But she hadn't realized how devoid of Josh the area looked with all of his personal items missing. It was as if he'd never been there.

She gazed at the stripped bed and barren bed-side table for a long moment. Then someone walked in through the doorway behind her. Julie wheeled around. What if it was one of the guys stopping by on the way to lunch? How could she explain what she was doing there? What if it was Gary again?

But it was only Lucinda carrying an armload of clean sheets. She smiled shyly at Julie and put the sheets on the night table so she could start making the bed.

"Su amigo?" she asked, her brown eyes sympathetic. Julie nodded sadly and suddenly Lucinda's face brightened. "I find this," she said haltingly, pulling a scrap of paper out of the pocket of her jeans. She handed the paper to Julie and then mimed how she'd found it under the edge of the mattress when she was taking off Josh's sheets.

Julie nodded to indicate that she understood. She thanked Lucinda and then looked down at the piece of paper in her hand. It could have been taken from Josh's notebook; there was a ragged left edge where the page had once been spirally bound. The block-printed words jumped out at her—*We'll talk tonight. I'll explain then.*

The top half of the page had been torn off, but Josh's scrawled signature at the upper right edge made it look as though he'd used the top part of the page to write a note. Whoever he'd written to had obviously printed a reply on the bottom half of the notebook page, torn off Josh's note at the top, and given the reply part to Josh, who'd no doubt stuffed it under the edge of his mattress.

Julie hurried from the room, clutching the scrap of paper. It was as if Josh had sent her a message and now she had to figure out what it meant.

Stopping in her own room, Julie opened a drawer of her bureau and carefully slid the note between the folds of her underwear. She wasn't sure what instinct made her keep the note a secret, but for now at least, she wasn't about to share its existence with anyone. Then she raced to the dining room for lunch.

During the afternoon ride Julie pondered the meaning of the note. Josh was always spying on people. And on that long ride the day of the rodeo, he'd hinted to her that he'd found out a number of secrets. He'd even said he'd give her a clue. Could this note be it? She shook her head decisively. It was only by chance that she'd been in his room and that Lucinda had found the note and given it to her. Besides, the note wasn't much of a clue. Anyone could have printed that short reply.

But the note could be telling her something else. Since it was under his mattress, that probably meant that someone had left the note in his room for him. *We'll talk tonight*. It could have been written at any time and been concealed under his mattress for days.

Then the thought suddenly struck her—had the note been left for Josh on Saturday? Had he been meeting the person who wrote it behind the rodeo chutes on Saturday night? Was that the reason he was there?

But that couldn't be right, she decided. Because if someone had been there when Josh fell or climbed into the bull's pen, that person would have helped Josh himself or gotten help from others. Unless . . . The idea pushed itself slowly but insistently into Julie's brain. She tried to deny it because the thought was too horrible to contemplate. Finally she could refuse it no longer. What if the person Josh was meeting had pushed him into that pen on purpose?

Julie shuddered as the rest of the knowledge came flooding to the surface of her mind. Someone had tried to kill Josh—he'd been incredibly lucky to be found alive—and that someone was certainly one of them at the ranch. Josh didn't know anyone else in Willow. Of course, she reasoned, he did know Pauline at the shelter and there were the shopkeepers that they'd talked to trying to get stuff for the playground. But she couldn't imagine that Josh knew anything about them that needed explaining. Besides, if she was right about the person leaving the note for Josh to find in his room, then it had to be someone at the ranch.

For Josh to have stuffed the note under his mattress might mean that he'd found it on his bed when he was in the room for only a few minutes, or when some of the other guys were around and he didn't want to draw attention to it by putting it away somewhere else. Otherwise he would probably have folded it inside his notebook.

The notebook! Why hadn't she thought of Josh's diary before? That had to be where Josh would leave her a clue to what he was doing. And Julie had had it in her hands just yesterday. She'd been an idiot to give it to Gary. She should have told him that the notebook was hers and taken it away with her to read.

As the group rode back toward the ranch, Julie knew what she had to do. Somehow she

must get the diary back. She was sure that if she
had the notebook, she would eventually know
what Josh knew, and then she might well know
who had tried to kill him.

As soon as she'd stowed Maggie's saddle and
brushed her glossy coat, Julie rushed into the
dining room hoping to find Ilene. No way was
she going to talk to Gary any more than she
absolutely had to, but Ilene seemed nice
enough, and Julie didn't know any other way to
find out what had become of Josh's stuff.

Luck was with her and Julie found Ilene and
Lucinda in the kitchen putting the finishing
touches on the evening meal. "Mmm, that
smells wonderful," Julie said as she entered the
kitchen.

Ilene smiled at her. "Well, I don't know if it's
the pork roast or the corn bread you smell, but
I hope you like it."

"I'm sure it'll all be great. You're a good
cook," Julie told her truthfully. "Anyway, Ilene,
I was wondering where Josh's duffel bag is."
She saw the puzzled look on the woman's face
and improvised quickly. "He had something of
mine and I think it must have gotten packed up
with his things."

"Oh, dear, that's too bad. What was it?"

Julie felt a moment of panic. She couldn't say

the diary belonged to her. What if Ilene mentioned it to Gary—he knew it wasn't hers. Her mind raced frantically, and then she remembered the key ring Josh was always fooling with. "It's a key ring, with a little magnifying glass attached to it. It's not all that valuable, but—"

"I know, sometimes little things are important," Ilene agreed. "But I don't know where the duffel bag is. I'm pretty sure it's not in the house, though—I'd have seen it. Gary must have put it in one of the outbuildings. Why don't you ask him?"

Trapped, Julie stared at the woman. The thought of talking to Gary about anything, and even worse, going off alone with him to find Josh's duffel bag, made her skin crawl. Finally she forced herself to smile. "It doesn't matter all that much—thanks anyway." She turned and made herself walk at a normal pace out of the kitchen.

That evening as Julie and Hannah were getting ready for bed, Hannah said a little sheepishly, "I didn't want to say anything before, but I've been kind of worried about the playground at the shelter." Then she grinned. "But now I think it's really going to work. The twins will probably get the swings done and up tomorrow, and if they deliver the sand for the sandbox . . ."

"Oh, I'd be surprised if they don't," Julie told her. "Nick's mom seems to be able to work magic, and if she says the sand is coming, it will be there."

Hannah laughed. "Yes, you're right. Well, anyway, the garden's ready to plant now. I hope you'll be able to help with that tomorrow. I'm sorry you got stuck inside painting today."

"Well, the painting's all done," Julie told her. "And it'll be good to be outside. Being shut up in a room with Pauline all morning isn't the most fun I've ever had." She smiled ruefully at Hannah. "I'm afraid I kind of put my foot in my mouth."

"She looked a little ticked off when she came out," Hannah agreed. "What happened?"

Julie repeated her conversation with Pauline to Hannah. She was a little surprised that the other girl didn't seem totally amazed by the sad tale. "I thought it must be something like that," Hannah said when Julie stopped talking. "Pauline is really lucky that the shelter exists and that she could get into it. And good for her for having the guts to get out of a dangerous situation. You wouldn't believe the stories I've heard about married women, some of them with young children, who are too afraid to leave husbands who beat them up. They live in fear for their lives."

For a moment both girls were silent. Then Julie said, "Well, I think Pauline's nuts. Here she's got a great guy like Nick who wants to be her friend, but she seems determined not to take the help he's offering. It's like she enjoys making things hard for herself."

"Oh, I don't think that's it at all," Hannah said. "You know, Julie, it's not so easy to take advice, even good advice. Sometimes you get so confused and scared that you think the only safe thing is to stay in the situation you're in, no matter what it is."

"Well, I still think she's an idiot to not even try to go to college. Besides, she'd be safer there. Her ex-boyfriend would never think of looking for her on a college campus, if that's what she's worried about."

Hannah smiled sadly. "Maybe she'll change her mind once she's thought it over some more. But it's hard to think clearly when you're in the middle of something. Sometimes it takes a complete change of scene to let some fresh ideas into your head."

Julie thought about what Hannah was saying. It was true that she probably wouldn't have had the space to take another look at her situation at home with Martha if she hadn't come to the ranch. And she guessed that Hannah had been doing some serious reevaluating of her own situation at home. From the little bit that Hannah had said, it sounded like she might have some heavy boyfriend problems.

Maybe what Josh had said when they first met at the airport was sort of right. Not that they'd been sent to the ranch because they'd done something wrong necessarily, but that they all had things to work out and could use the distance from home to get a new perspective.

Julie wondered what had troubled Josh. She glanced at the bureau drawer where she'd put the note Lucinda had given her. Julie had decided not to tell anyone at all about her suspicions until she had more information. But now, in the cozy intimacy of their shared bedroom, she wanted to confide in Hannah.

Slowly Julie got up and went to the bureau. She extracted the note and looked over at the other girl. "Hannah," she said at last, "I think someone tried to kill Josh."

It was a relief to pour out her fears and to voice her speculations aloud. Hannah listened in silence to the entire recital, a mixture of horror and disbelief on her face.

"But you're saying it was one of us, that one of us wanted to kill Josh," Hannah said when Julie was finished. "I mean, I can see how you could come to that conclusion, but really, Julie, it's awfully hard to believe."

They were both silent, pondering the idea that one of their group had done something so horrible. Even to let him die in an accident without saying anything or trying to find help was beyond imagination. Finally Hannah asked, "Who could it be?"

Suddenly Julie knew the answer. "Roy," she said. "It's got to be him. He and Josh were always at each other's throats. And Josh was really trying to find out what Roy was doing when we were all working at the shelter. Maybe he did. And maybe he asked Roy for an explanation and a push into the bullpen was Roy's answer."

"Oh, no," Hannah said slowly, shaking her head. "I don't believe Roy would do something like that." She saw the determined look on Julie's face and went on. "I know he acts a little strange sometimes—"

"A little strange!" Julie exclaimed. "Are you kidding me? He and Josh had a fistfight. I'm sure it's true, even if neither one of them admitted it. And he's always sneaking off. He tried to kill Josh to keep his secret from being known. And when I get Josh's diary, I'm going to have proof!"

"But, Julie, even if he and Josh did get into a

fight, that's a whole lot different from attempted murder. And I can't imagine that Roy's secret is so important that he'd do something like that."

"Well, maybe he didn't plan to kill Josh. Maybe it was an accident. But then he let Josh lie there while everyone searched for him and never said a word."

Hannah looked at Julie's face. It was flushed with anger. "Look, let's sleep on it," Hannah suggested. "It's late and we're both tired." She saw Julie about to protest and went on. "You've been stewing over this note all day. Besides, there's nothing we can do about it now. Maybe we'll see things a little differently by tomorrow."

Right, Julie thought, what she really means is that I'll have changed my mind by tomorrow. But I won't.

When she turned off her light to go to sleep, Julie was sorry she'd confided in Hannah. What had made her think that Hannah would understand and be helpful? But the next morning, Julie woke up with a slightly different attitude. Even if Hannah needed some convincing about Roy's guilt, at least Julie had someone to talk to about it. She hadn't realized what a terrible burden her suspicions were. She'd done the right thing by sharing them with the other girl. Now there were two of them to figure out a way to get the diary, and two of them to keep a watch on Roy.

CHAPTER

FIFTEEN

As they were leaving for breakfast Hannah said, "I've been thinking. Maybe we ought to talk to the sheriff about this. If you're right about Roy, then we shouldn't be trying to handle this alone."

"Right," Julie said sarcastically. "And just what are we going to tell the sheriff? That I've got some kind of lamebrain idea just from six words on a scrap of paper?"

"Well, if we talk to the cops, then they can find out what Roy's been up to—it'll be their problem to deal with."

"No way," Julie exclaimed in alarm. "You've got to promise not to say anything about this to anybody. If you even breathe one word, Roy is bound to find out. We're a lot safer if he doesn't know we suspect a thing. We've got to wait until we have some kind of proof."

"Yeah, you're right," Hannah admitted glumly. "Cops are terrible blabbermouths. It was a stupid idea."

What makes her such an expert on cops? Julie wondered fleetingly. Then she said, "Just act totally natural. It's our best defense."

Hannah nodded. "Okay. I promise, I won't say a word to anyone. I won't even think it."

For once, when they got to the minivan, Julie didn't care that Roy had already seated himself up front next to Nick. In fact she was relieved. She and Hannah climbed in all the way to the back and Julie was glad that she could keep an eye on Roy without being watched in return. She'd gone out of her way to avoid him during breakfast and she didn't know how she'd respond if she had to deal with him directly. Knowing that he'd been responsible for Josh's injuries—even if it had been an accident, which she doubted—made her look at everything Roy did and said with suspicion.

When they arrived at the shelter, they discovered that the load of clean sand and a couple of large tarpaulins had been left outside the gate to the playground. Pauline rounded up a wheelbarrow and shovel and then went to help the twins finish the swings. Roy tagged after Hannah as she gathered the garden supplies over near the plot they'd dug up the day before.

Happy to be left alone with Nick, Julie helped him move in the sand to fill the giant tractor tire. "Pauline told me yesterday that you're trying to help her get into college," Julie said to him. "I think she's crazy not to jump at the chance." She gave Nick what she hoped was an engaging smile. "You sure wouldn't have to ask me twice."

Nick returned her smile with a wry one of his one. "You don't need my help," he said.

Julie laughed. "Don't be silly. I'd take all the help I could get."

"Julie, be serious," Nick said. "You've got everything a girl could want. You're pretty and smart and capable. And I'm sure you've got lots of boyfriends. Nice boyfriends. Pauline's not as lucky as you are." He paused for a moment and then said, "I wish she'd agree to let me help her. She needs to get her life back on track."

Basking in the warm glow of his compliments, Julie said earnestly, "I agree. And I did my best to talk her into going away to school. But I don't think I succeeded."

Nick sighed. "Yeah, me neither. And I don't know how to make her look at things in another way."

"Why don't you introduce her to your mom?"

Julie suggested. "Etta seems like someone who could talk anyone into anything." As soon as the words were out of her mouth, Julie regretted them. It had been one thing to suggest to Pauline that she ask Nick's mom to help her get a job. Pauline was so determined not to be a burden to anyone that she was unlikely to actually get in touch with Etta. But for Julie to tell Nick to hook Pauline up with his mom was lunacy. She was practically pushing Pauline into being part of Nick's family.

Nick looked thoughtful for a moment and then he said, "That's a really good idea. You know, Julie, you're terrific." He gave her a big grin and Julie's heart soared. I'll bet Nick isn't interested in Pauline at all and just wants to be her friend, she decided.

Julie was so involved with talking to Nick and with putting together the sandbox that an hour or so had gone by before she even looked around to see what everyone else was doing. She had noticed Roy going over to the garden area with Hannah earlier and hoped that the other girl was okay with that. But they were safe enough all outside together. Besides, Roy would have slipped away as soon as things got going. So she wasn't surprised to see Hannah all alone on her hands and knees planting little seedlings in the garden patch.

I need to go and help her, Julie thought guilt-
ily. She covered the sandbox with the tarp and
then headed toward the garden area. The
swings were in place, and on the way, Julie
couldn't resist sitting in one and giving herself
a push. As the swing flew up in the air, a voice
from behind Julie gave her a start.

"You planning on flying off on that thing?" It
was Roy!

Julie dragged her feet on the ground and
pulled herself to a stop. Roy leaned against the
tree trunk smiling at her. "What are you doing
here?" Julie demanded, keeping her voice low
so that Nick wouldn't hear her. "I thought you
always had some secret project of your own to
work on."

"Well, not today," Roy said matter-of-factly.
"I'm helping the twins build that contraption
over there."

Julie looked in the direction Roy indicated.
She knew that the twins had come up with some
sort of idea for a climbing construction. Now
she saw that they had roped together a barrel
and a ladder and a bunch of blocks of wood.
Nick was standing near the thing conferring
with the twins. "You'd better get back to work,
then," Julie said to Roy in as even a tone as she
could manage. Then she forced herself to walk

toward the garden area without a backward glance.

On the way back to the ranch they stopped again at the hospital. Josh didn't look any different today. Julie looked around for a doctor or nurse she could ask about his progress. But the nurse on duty was obviously extremely busy, and before Julie could find anyone else, Nick hustled everyone back out to the minivan. At least he isn't worse, she reassured herself.

That afternoon, when they went out to saddle the horses, Gary appeared to help. He checked out Hannah's horse and then walked over to Julie. As he ran his hands over the saddle and bridle to make sure they were on correctly, he said, "I'm glad to see that all of you are getting back into the swing of things. It's too bad about your friend, but accidents do happen." He gave Julie a steady look and then returned his attention to the horse. "I was worried about you kids. You especially, Julie. Josh is a special friend of yours, isn't he?"

"Yes, he is," Julie said through clenched teeth. Then she grabbed Maggie's reins and walked away, pulling the horse behind her. He's such a creep, Julie thought as she reached up and patted Maggie's neck. She glanced quickly over her shoulder and saw that Gary was watching her.

Toward the end of dinner that evening, Gary walked into the dining room. What now? Julie wondered. It seemed that Gary only appeared at meals when he had some sort of pronouncement to make. And this time was no exception.

"I've just been talking to Mrs. Fremont," he told them. "We've decided to move your solo ride up one day. So you'll go out day after tomorrow and then you'll have Friday to just relax and hang out at the ranch. You've been working very hard at that shelter in town and you deserve a break. So finish everything up tomorrow morning and then you might want to discuss your solo riding plans with Nick in the afternoon. He can get you organized so that you each have a separate route up to the summer hut."

"Wow," Hannah said to Julie. "Good thing we got so much done in the garden today."

"Yeah," Julie agreed. "But I don't know whether that thing the twins want to build is going to get finished. I think they're going to have to simplify their plans."

When they'd finished eating, Roy pushed back his chair and said something about a ball game he wanted to watch on TV. Julie watched him slouch off toward the living room with a sigh of relief. It was hard enough to pretend she didn't know he was a would-be killer when she didn't have to talk to him. But mealtimes were now very difficult.

The twins looked as though they were ready to leave, too, but Julie stopped them. "Could we just talk about that thing you're building at the shelter?" she asked. "I'm worried that it won't get done tomorrow."

As the two boys described their project Julie could tell from their expressions that they, too, suspected they couldn't finish in one day.

"You've got a barrel for them to crawl through. Why don't you leave it at that?" Hannah suggested.

"But that's so dumb," Brian protested.

"It's like nothing," Bret agreed.

They all sat there thinking for a few minutes. Then Julie said, "I've got an idea. Since you've already figured out how to mount a teeter-totter, why don't you use the ladder for that instead of a plain board and put it on top of the barrel? If you make seats for the ends of the ladder . . ." She jumped up from the table. "Let me get a piece of paper and a pencil and I'll show you what I mean."

The four of them spent almost an hour re-working Julie's idea. But by the time they were done, they all agreed that the contraption would work. And best of all, it wouldn't take very long to put together.

The sky was still light, even at nine o'clock in the evening. "Let's go for a walk or something," Hannah said. "I'm not ready to go back to the room."

The twins had gone to watch TV with Roy, and Julie thought, This is the perfect opportunity to poke around and see if we can figure out where Gary put Josh's duffel bag. She stopped and looked around. No one was in sight, and she quickly said in an undertone, "Let's go exploring—maybe we can find Josh's diary."

They stopped in the barn, but the stalls held only saddles and other tack. Climbing the narrow stairs to the hayloft, they could see there was no place to store a duffel bag. The barn cat met them as they came back down, and they stopped to pet her and admire her roly-poly kittens. One tried to walk across the old blanket that was their bed, and the girls laughed as it toppled in a heap.

In the doorway Julie stood and gazed across the corral. What were those three small buildings used for? She had no idea, but perhaps one of them was for storage. "Come on," she urged Hannah, "let's go over there."

Two of the buildings were practically falling

down, with doors sagging on their hinges and nothing inside but old junk. The third one, however, was in much better shape—and its door was secured with a padlock. "This must be it," Julie breathed. She pulled at the lock, but it didn't open. Frustrated, she walked around to the side of the building as Hannah followed.

The grimy glass of the small window was cracked. The girls peered in, cupping their hands around their eyes to block reflections. But, though there was still plenty of light outside, the interior was shrouded in shadow. It was impossible to identify anything in the inky darkness.

"We'll have to come back in the daytime," Julie said in a low voice. Then she clutched Hannah's arm and they both froze.

"Okay, then, that's about it." It was Gary!

The girls stared at each other. Had he seen them? But then another voice said something they couldn't distinguish, and they realized he'd been calling to one of the ranch hands.

Then he said loudly, "Don't worry, I'll check it out." He was much nearer now. He must be coming to the shed!

"We've got to get out of here," Julie whispered urgently.

"Which way?"

They could hear his footsteps now, swishing through the grass. He was probably going to the door of the shed, and the two of them crept silently around the corner to the back of the little building. Stopping, they listened, their hearts pounding wildly. When the rattle of the padlock told them he'd reached the door, they glanced quickly at one another and then bolted for the safety of the house.

Racing into their room, they shut the door and leaned against it, breathing so hard they couldn't speak. But Julie knew that Hannah was thinking the same thing she was. Had Gary seen them? And what would they say if he asked what they thought they were doing out at the shed?

CHAPTER

SIXTEEN

Julie and Hannah were grateful that Gary didn't make an appearance at breakfast the next day. They were still nervous, but at least any questions he might ask had been postponed. At the shelter they checked the progress of their garden while the twins explained to Nick and Roy what their new plan was. Nick went off in the minivan, saying he'd be back as soon as he could. Meanwhile Brian and Bret began sanding pieces of wood for seesaw seats.

As soon as Nick had gone, Roy sauntered into the shelter. Julie crept in behind him and saw him go out the front door. "Well, Roy's gone again," she told Hannah. "The least he could have done was help out on this last day. But I guess you can't expect a killer to be thoughtful."

Hannah was trickling water from the hose onto the new plants. "You know, the more I think about it, the more difficult it is to believe that Roy had anything to do with Josh's accident," she said.

"You're too softhearted," Julie said. "You just don't want to believe that someone you know could do something like that. Not even someone who acts as strange as Roy."

"Well, that's just it. He does act strange. But not the way you mean. It's almost as if there's something he's embarrassed about, even ashamed of."

Julie snorted. "I'd say trying to kill another kid is definitely something to be ashamed about." She glared at Hannah. "Don't you care about what happened to Josh?"

"Of course I do," Hannah said. "It's just that I'm not sure your answer is the right one."

"Right," Julie said in total disagreement. "Come on, let's see if we can help the twins."

Hannah was shaking her head as she turned off the hose. "They don't need any help," she told Julie. "I've already asked them. Actually, I think they want this to be their project and would just as soon we stayed out of it. Why don't we go to the library and see if we can get some books for the kids? Those new shelves look awfully empty."

They walked through the pleasant tree-lined

streets of Willow. Julie couldn't get over Hannah's naïveté in believing that Roy hadn't left Josh to die. But she realized that she herself was more and more thinking of it as an accident. Still, even if that were the case, Julie couldn't forgive Roy's blatant lies on Saturday night when he said he hadn't seen Josh.

When they got to the library, they found it remarkably well stocked for such a small town. The children's room was on the lower level and a bunch of little kids were sitting on the floor listening to one of the librarians read a story. "Look how enthralled they are," Julie whispered.

"Sure," Hannah said softly. "Don't you remember how wonderful it was when you were little and your parents read to you every night?"

The two girls crept around gathering books that looked interesting until they each had an armful. "I hope they'll let us check them out," Julie said as they started for the stairs to the main floor.

Hannah said, "Oh, it'll probably be okay. We'll tell them the books are for the shelter and we'll ask Pauline to make sure they get returned."

Ahead of them was a small office. A woman sat at the desk inside and a guy was sitting with his back toward them. Julie jabbed Hannah with her elbow. "That looks like Roy!"

He must have heard her, and it was Roy. He whirled around in his chair, then raced out of the office and up the stairs. The woman still sat at her desk, looking first at Roy's retreating figure and then at Julie and Hannah. Her look of annoyance turned into a frown of disapproval, and Julie changed her mind about stopping to ask what Roy had been doing there.

When the two girls got to the top of the stairs, Roy was nowhere in sight. "Boy, was that weird," Julie said.

Hannah looked thoughtful but didn't comment. Instead she began to explain to the woman at the checkout desk what they wanted to do with the books.

On their way back to the shelter, Julie asked, "What in the world was Roy doing at the library?"

"Who knows? Maybe he wanted to check out some books. But even you can't build a visit to the library into something sinister."

The encounter piqued Julie's curiosity, but she disliked the idea of talking to Roy too much to ask him. In any case, he didn't show up until they were almost ready to leave. Without even a glance at Julie and Hannah, Roy headed toward the twins to inspect their project.

Pauline came out to look at the garden. "This is great," she told Julie and Hannah. "Can't you guys come back tomorrow? You should get a chance to see the kids enjoying all this stuff."

Julie shook her head. She was disappointed, too. Then Hannah said suddenly, "Why don't we come on Friday? Gary said we'd have the day to ourselves to do what we want. And what I want to do is come back here and watch the kids have a good time."

"Great!" Pauline said. "We'll make lots of food and have a picnic here in the yard. It'll be fun."

Before they left they tried out the teeter-totter-and-barrel construction. It worked perfectly and Julie noticed the twins standing side by side, beaming with pride.

They stopped again at the hospital and stood outside Josh's room, watching the green blips moving across the screen. Hearing footsteps behind her, Julie turned to see a woman in a white coat walking along the hall. "Excuse me," Julie said without pausing to think, "are you the doctor?"

"Yes?" The woman's voice made the word a brisk question.

"Well, we're Josh's friends"—Julie gestured toward the boy's still form lying in the bed—

"and I was wondering, um, is he going to be okay? I mean, do you think he's going to wake up?"

The doctor smiled sympathetically. "I know you're all worried about him. We can't make any promises; these things are hard to predict. But he does seem to be responding better, and we don't think there is major brain damage."

"Oh!" Julie felt as though a weight had been lifted from her shoulders. She saw that the rest of the kids were listening intently.

"We're hoping he may regain consciousness in another day or two," the doctor said. "But don't expect him to be up and around right away—he had some pretty serious injuries." She included them all in her smile, and then walked quickly toward the nurses' station.

A buzz of excited talk rose from the group as they left the hospital. In spite of the doctor's first cautious words, Julie couldn't keep the happiness from bubbling up inside her. Josh was going to be all right! Then, as the minivan bumped along the road to the ranch, she thought, When he wakes up, Josh can tell us what happened that night at the bullpen. And he could explain whatever clues he'd written in his diary. Julie was relieved to realize that now she wouldn't need to keep searching for Josh's notebook.

After lunch, Julie was dismayed to see Gary in the corral, helping Nick saddle the horses. "Why don't you take them up through Diablo Canyon?" Gary was saying. "You haven't been up that way yet, have you?"

Nick shook his head. "No, but I thought the rain last week might have washed out some of the trail."

"Naw," Gary assured him. "I was just up there yesterday and it's fine." He gave Maggie's rump a slap, then glanced over his shoulder and flashed a strange half smile at Julie. Then he turned and walked away. Julie breathed a sigh of relief and quickly mounted her horse.

Gary was still talking to Nick. "These kids are getting to be pretty good riders. Old Diablo Canyon will be a sort of challenge for them."

"Challenge" was hardly the word for it, Julie thought as the little band made its way up a steep slope and then turned onto a narrow trail halfway up a canyon. Nick was in front and Julie had maneuvered herself into a position right behind him. José and Bob took up the rear.

The trail was nothing more than a narrow shelf carved into the side of a steep canyon wall. On her right, Julie's leg was practically rubbing against the rock surface that shot straight up. On the other side, she could look down for what seemed like miles. Tall pines covered the gentler slopes below, but up here there were only scruffy little bushes and a few small trees sticking out from cracks in the rock.

"This part is a little tricky," Nick called back over his shoulder. "We come to a plateau with a beautiful view up ahead. But in the meantime, don't try to be heroes. Just hang on to your saddle horns. The horses know the way."

Julie peered over at the almost sheer drop so close to her horse's feet. She hadn't needed any encouragement from Nick. Her hands were already gripping the saddle horn so tightly that her knuckles were white. She hadn't known before that she was afraid of heights, but it was painfully obvious to her now.

"Good going, Maggie girl," she crooned softly. "You're doing a great job." Slowly Julie unclenched one hand from the saddle horn and gently patted the horse's neck. "Just keep it up," she urged.

They wound around another bend and Julie could glimpse the near edge of the plateau a short distance away. Not much farther to go, she said to herself with relief.

Then, as Julie adjusted herself slightly in her saddle, everything went wrong. The saddle began sliding off the center of Maggie's back, tilting Julie out over the edge of the trail. Julie leaned toward the rock wall on her right to try to compensate for the shift of the saddle. But once moved off center, the saddle continued to slide.

Although it took only seconds of real time, it seemed to Julie as if it were all happening in slow motion. The saddle slipping around toward the horse's belly, her own desperate attempt to right it, then her realization that she was falling. The sheer drop came up to meet her as she hit the ground and then bounced toward the edge of the narrow trail.

"Nick!" she screamed as she flailed her arms, trying to hold on to anything solid to keep from falling into the canyon below. That was certain death, she knew, and her fingers grabbed at the surface of the trail itself. But all she could get hold of were handfuls of dirt and little bits of rock.

She felt her feet go over first, with nothing under them now but air. Then the rest of her body began to follow.

Julie kicked her feet, looking for a toehold, anything to stop her fall. They caught at a bush, but it gave way under her, its puny roots easily dislodged from a crack in the rock surface. Then the toe of her boot found another crack and she jammed her foot into it as far as she could. "Nick!" she screamed again.

And suddenly there he was, his body lying prone on the trail and his face leaning over in front of hers. His strong hands grasped Julie's arms. "You're okay," he said. "I've got you."

By the time Nick, assisted by José, dragged Julie back up to the trail, she was shaking so hard she could barely stand. One sleeve of her western shirt was torn and her face and hands were scratched, but miraculously there was no real damage. The sturdy denim of her jeans and her cowboy boots had taken the brunt of the scraping fall and had emerged almost unscathed.

After making sure that there were no broken bones or sprains, Nick said to her, "It's too narrow here for us to turn around and go back. We'll have to go on to the plateau." He looked at her with concern in his eyes. "How do you feel about that?"

Julie felt tears staining her cheeks. "Not great," was her mumbled answer. She could see that there was no alternative but to go forward. But the thought of getting back on her horse was too scary to contemplate. Of course it hadn't been Maggie's fault that the saddle's cinch strap had come loose. The gentle beast stood steady as a rock, blinking in the afternoon sun, and Julie imagined that even those big brown eyes looked worried.

After a few more gulps of air to steady herself, Julie said, "I'll be okay. But I think I'll walk the rest of the way." She turn to pat Maggie's neck and then said to the horse, "You were a good girl and I hope you're not offended, but I just can't get back up on you right now."

"Oh, no, of course not," Nick said quickly, correctly interpreting Julie's words to her horse as an explanation to him. "You'll ride with me. Rocky can carry both of us just fine."

Before Julie could protest, he mounted his horse and then took his foot out of the stirrup so that Julie could use it to climb up on the big animal's back. José stood behind her to help, and in a moment she was sitting on the horse's bare back behind Nick's saddle. "Just put your arms around my waist and hang on to me," Nick told her. "I won't let anything happen to you."

"What about Maggie?"

"Oh, she'll follow along. Don't worry."

Julie looked over her shoulder at her horse standing just behind Nick's and then to the stricken faces of the other kids still astride their own horses. José and Bob must have told them to stay on their horses when she fell, and from

the looks on their faces, they weren't about to
get off anyway.

They rode the hundred yards or so to the
broad plateau and then came to a stop in a little
group. José reached up and grabbed Julie to
help her down, and when her feet hit the
ground, she starting shaking again. Hannah
jumped off her horse and ran to Julie, throwing
her arms around the other girl. "Are you okay?"
Hannah asked breathlessly. She felt Julie's
trembling and led her to a big flat rock nearby.
"Here, sit down."

"I couldn't believe it when I saw you falling,"
Hannah went on. "It was like a nightmare come
true. You must have been terrified."

"I still am," Julie told her, and attempted a
little laugh. "I guess I won't forget my ride
through Diablo Canyon for a while."

"None of us will," Hannah assured her.
"Those poor horses are going to have their
cinch straps so tight on the way back that they'll
hardly be able to breathe."

Bob came over with a canteen of water and
Julie took several grateful swallows. She could
see Nick busily checking the other horses and
fiddling with all the saddles. His face was grim
with determination and every now and then he
threw a worried look in Julie's direction.

"Poor Nick," Julie said to Hannah when Bob had left. "He acts as though it was his fault."

Hannah snorted. "Poor Nick, baloney. He should have double-checked those saddles before we left the ranch."

"But it was just an accident," Julie protested. Though she was still shaking with residual fear from her fall, her first instinct was to protect Nick. And after all, he'd saved her. If it hadn't been for his quick action . . . She shuddered again at the memory.

"Well, I guess you can be generous-minded if you want to be," Hannah said. "You're the person who almost took a one-way trip to oblivion. But I'm not sure I'd feel the same way."

Julie gave her a little smile. "I'm not blaming Nick. But I think Gary doesn't have the brains he was born with. He's the one who told Nick to take us on this trail."

"That slimebag," Hannah said with disgust. Then she hugged Julie again. "The important thing is that you're okay."

At that point Nick came over to where the two girls were sitting. He scuffed his boot toe in the dirt and seemed unable to look either girl in the eye. "I'm really sorry about that, Julie," he began.

"Hey, accidents happen," she said with as

much bravado as she could muster. "And I'm fine now, thanks to you."

"Well, the bad news is that we have to go back the same way we came in." He sort of mumbled the words and flinched as soon as they'd left his mouth, as if expecting hysterical shrieks from both Julie and Hannah. He waited for a moment and then went on. "I know it's not comfortable riding double with me, but I'd appreciate it if you could manage. I want to make sure you're safe for the rest of this trip and the only way I can do that is to keep you on my horse with me."

Julie looked at him and caught his eyes with hers. This time her smile was genuine. "Oh, I think I can manage that okay," she said.

For everyone else, the trip back to the ranch was totally uneventful. But for Julie it was practically a dream come true. *I wish I hadn't had to almost get myself killed to be in this position,* she thought wryly. Still, riding behind Nick with her arms snugly around his waist and leaning against his firm back was worth every scary moment. In her mind's eye she could see the two of them riding off into the sunset together.

She savored the long ride back to the ranch and was sorry when it came to an end. But she loved the look on Gary's face when they stopped in front of the barn. His mouth hung open in surprise when he spotted Julie clinging to Nick on top of Rocky. As he raced over to ask what had happened, Julie thought, Hannah's right, you really are a slimeball. I'll bet you're worried sick that my parents are going to sue the pants off you for putting me in this danger.

Actually, she guessed her dad would be right on the phone to his lawyers if Julie called him in hysterics. But of course, that would get Nick in trouble, too, something she really didn't want to happen. So, ignoring Gary's questions, she leaned against Nick as he put his arm around her shoulders and walked her to her room.

Gary tried to follow them into the room, but Hannah was too quick for him. She cut Gary off, maneuvering herself inside with Julie and Nick, and then turned to face Gary in the doorway. "Julie needs to rest now," she told Gary, and happily slammed the door in his face.

CHAPTER

SEVENTEEN

Hannah listened at the door for a few moments until the sound of Gary's receding footsteps convinced her that he wouldn't try to come in again. Then she looked over at Julie and Nick. Julie was lying on the bed and Nick was sitting on its edge holding her hand. "Well, I think I'll take a shower," Hannah announced, and walked into the bathroom.

When she came out, Nick was gone. Julie lay on her bed, tears streaking her cheeks. "What's wrong?" Hannah asked with concern. "Just now getting a reaction to your fall?"

"Maybe," Julie said with a sniffle. Then she blurted out, "He's got a girlfriend."

Ever practical, Hannah asked, "How do you know?"

"He told me." Julie sniffled some more. "He was saying how grateful he was that I didn't blame him for the accident and how sorry he was that it had happened. Then he told me that if something like that happened to his girlfriend at college, he'd probably kill the guy who was responsible."

Hannah sank down on the edge of the bed where Nick had been sitting earlier. "Hey, it can't be all that hot a romance if she's his college girlfriend and he doesn't see her all summer. Besides, before long you'll be back in L.A." She took Julie's hand and grinned at her. "I'll grant you he's cute, but there are lots of cute guys in the world. And none of them are cute enough to cry over."

After a bit Hannah convinced Julie to take a long soaking bath, once again liberally dosing the water with expensive bath oil. Then Julie lay down on her bed and drifted off to sleep while Hannah sat in the easy chair in their room and read. She didn't feel right about leaving Julie alone, although Julie hadn't specifically asked her to stay.

There was something dangerous in the atmosphere at the ranch. Hannah couldn't explain her unease in any sort of logical terms, but she knew enough to listen to her instincts. She remembered the last time she hadn't paid attention to her own inner voice; there had been serious consequences. She hoped that she'd learned something since then.

Soon there was a soft knock on the door and Hannah opened it to find Brian, Bret, and Roy standing in the hallway. "We wanted to see how Julie is," Brian said.

"Yes, we don't want to disturb her, but is she coming to dinner?" Bret added.

Julie stirred on the bed and slowly opened her eyes. "Gosh, I was out like a light," she said, and stretched.

Hannah said, "The guys are here asking if you're going to dinner. What do you think?"

"Are you kidding? I could eat a horse," Julie said. "All I need to do is pull on some clothes and I'll be there."

Hannah grinned at the three boys, who had obviously heard Julie's reply. "We'll be right along."

The fright of the afternoon ride had stimulated both Julie's appetite and everyone else's admiration for her. Even Roy was more forthcoming than usual. "I don't know how you got back up on a horse after what happened," he said in awe. "I was feeling sick the whole way back, and I'm not the one who fell."

Finishing the last of her huge bowl of stew, Julie sank back in her chair. "Wow, what a day," she said. "First the great news about Josh, and then the scariest event of my life."

Ilene turned away from the sideboard where she'd been setting out the dessert. "What's this about Josh?"

Several of them spoke at once, explaining what the doctor had said. "Well, that really is good news," Ilene said. "I'll have to tell Gary."

By the time dinner was over, Julie was feeling pretty cocky. But then Brian asked the question no one else had been willing to voice. "Are you going on the solo ride tomorrow?"

Julie's euphoric bubble burst. "I don't know," she said slowly. "I guess I should." She looked at Hannah as if asking advice.

"There's plenty of time to decide on that," Hannah said breezily. "It wouldn't be so bad if you canceled out. I can't imagine that anyone thinks you ought to go."

"But last week you said it's important to get back up on a horse and ride after you've had a scare. You made it sound like someone would be psychologically damaged for life if they didn't," Julie said.

Hannah brushed her own words of wisdom aside. "That's for when you've had a little fright, not when you've almost gotten killed." She looked at Julie sympathetically. "You're the only one who can decide, and no one is going to blame you if you just sit at the ranch all day and read a book. Why don't you see how you feel in the morning, after a good night's sleep?"

Suddenly a loud clap of thunder startled them all. Rain began to fall and dark clouds blotted out the evening sun. "That storm may make the decision for all of us," Roy said as they stared out the dining-room windows at the downpour. "If it's slippery and muddy, I don't think Gary will let us go. Especially not after what happened to Julie this afternoon. He won't want to take a chance."

"Oh, I don't know," Brian said, disagreeing. "These summer rains come and go pretty quickly, and it's dry here, so the ground soaks up the water fast."

"We did a weather section in natural-science class last year," Bret explained. "The Rockies are famous for storms that arrive out of nowhere and then disappear."

"Well, I'm not going to try and wait it out," Hannah said. "Come on, Julie, let's grab some dessert to take to our room and get out of here before it gets worse."

In the coziness of their room the girls ate in companionable silence. After a while Julie said, "Thanks for staying with me this afternoon. I don't think I'd have been able to sleep if I'd been all alone."

"No big deal," Hannah told her. "We're here to please."

"Right," Julie said with a laugh. "In that case, let me see if I can come up with some more requests." After a moment she went on, "You know, Roy was awfully sweet tonight. And he seemed pretty happy when he heard Josh is going to be okay. I don't understand it. Doesn't he realize that when Josh wakes up, he'll explain everything and then everyone will know Roy tried to kill him?"

Hannah sighed. "I think you're wrong about Roy, Julie. He's not the type of guy who gets into that kind of trouble. Belligerent, yes. Sullen, yes. Even a little hot under the collar, I'll grant you. But he doesn't seem like someone who could do anything truly violent, and he's certainly not a good enough liar to pretend it didn't happen."

"Oh, yeah?" Julie said. "So where do you get all this insight into human behavior? Are you some kind of expert on troubled teens, or what?"

Hannah blushed and looked down at her lap, her fingers picking at an invisible spot on her robe. "Well, you could say that, I guess," she said slowly. "I got into a lot of trouble last year, and it was mostly because I didn't pay attention to what I've known about people all along."

Now she had Julie's undivided attention. "What happened?"

Once she got started, it didn't take Hannah long to spill out the whole story. Her dad had come into a lot of money a few years back because of some invention he'd come up with. So the family moved to an upscale community in Connecticut. Hannah tried too hard to make friends and ended up running around with a bunch of rich kids who thought breaking into houses and stealing stuff was a blast.

"Larry?" Julie asked, remembering the cute guy from home Hannah had said earlier was big trouble.

Hannah nodded. "He was pretty much the ringleader and I don't think any of the rest of us would have done that stuff if he hadn't made it sound sort of like a joke, or a dare."

"Some joke," Julie commented.

"Yeah, and I knew better. We all did. But we went along anyway. And of course eventually we got caught."

"What did they do to you? Did you have to go to jail?" Julie asked.

"No, we were pretty lucky. The juvenile-court

judge was a nice lady and she gave us community-service work to do and said that if we didn't get into any more trouble, the arrest would be wiped off our records."

Hannah stopped, tears filling her eyes. "The biggest problem was with my folks. They were really upset. They blamed themselves for not seeing what was going on, and now they're thinking of moving again so I can get a fresh start at some other school." She buried her face in her hands. "Oh, Julie, it's been a nightmare, the whole thing."

Julie got up from her bed and perched on the arm of Hannah's chair. She put her hand on the other girl's shoulder. "Hey, everyone makes mistakes. I mean, if we don't have mistakes to learn from, how are we supposed to know anything?"

Hannah laughed through her tears. "I should take you home with me so you could explain that to my folks. I'm sure we could all benefit from your take on things."

The next morning dawned bright and beautiful. True to the twins' prediction, the rain had come and gone, leaving behind a fresh dewiness in the air but very little mud.

Gary showed up in the dining room during breakfast and Julie was thankful again that he hadn't hovered around her at dinner the night before. Now that she thought about it, it was a little strange that he hadn't made a fuss about her near-death experience on the ride. But perhaps he wanted to keep things low-key in the hopes that Julie wouldn't view it as a big deal. Or maybe Hannah's slamming the door in his face was all it took. Julie would have to compliment Hannah on that tactic.

"I've been talking with Mrs. Fremont, and she's very pleased to hear about Josh's progress. We also discussed the solo ride scheduled for today," Gary began.

Julie was getting plenty tired of hearing Gary begin his pronouncements by ascribing them to a conversation with Mrs. Fremont. Why didn't she come in and tell them this stuff herself? Then Julie thought of the poor woman having all these heart-to-heart discussions with odious Gary. That sure wouldn't be any fun. Still, she was a grown person and she was the one who'd hired him.

"Our first decision was to shorten the ride," Gary went on. "No telling what damage last night's storm caused farther up in the mountains, so we don't want you to ride to the summer hut. And we don't want to take a chance on your getting caught in another storm late this afternoon or this evening. So our plan is to have you leave midmorning with a packed lunch and to be back here by midafternoon." He looked around the group as if trying to tell how this idea was going over.

"But in light of yesterday's accident, I'm now wondering if you want to go at all. What do you say?" he asked.

The rest of the kids turned to Julie. It was clear that they all were looking forward to this final adventure but somehow felt guilty about saying so in front of her. Before she knew what she was doing, Julie said, "I want to go. I think it sounds great."

Everyone at the table broke into enthusiastic chatter, both in relief that the ride was on and gratitude to Julie for getting them out of a sticky situation.

"Well, that settles it," Gary said when they'd quieted down. "Now, Lucinda has stayed home from work today because her mother is sick, so Ilene will make your lunches and you can come in and get them before you leave."

When they got out to the barn, full of eager anticipation, Nick was sitting on a bale of straw with a big topographical map spread across his lap. "Are you sure you feel up to this?" he asked Julie.

Julie nodded as the rest of them gathered round. "Okay, then I need to talk to each of you individually before you head out," Nick told them. "After that I'm going to draw your routes on the map so everyone understands where everyone else is going."

He looked up at them, his expression brooking no argument. "This is not a treasure hunt or some other secretive maneuver. It's supposed to be a time for each of you to be by yourselves for a while, not a time for anyone to get into trouble. We've had enough already." He paused and went on. "Bob and José and I need to know where you'll be and we'll be riding around checking on you the whole time."

"That's not my concept of being by myself," Roy complained. "I thought the whole idea was to be off on our own."

"It is," Nick assured him. "We won't interrupt what you're doing. And we won't tell anyone what we see. We'll keep our distance, but we have to make sure you're all safe." He grinned at Roy and then at the rest of them. "Actually we always check up on kids when they ride out alone. It's just that we don't usually say so, and nobody ever knows we're there. But, because you all might be a little nervous after yesterday's experience, I think it's good for you to know that we'll be around."

After glancing at each of their faces to make sure everyone got the message, Nick sent them off to saddle their horses. Then he started with Julie. "I don't know where you had in mind to go, but I've come up with something that I think you'll feel fairly secure with," he told her. "It's not far up in the hills, it's not steep or danger-ous, and you can almost see the ranch the whole time you're gone."

Julie watched as Nick drew a line on the map and then pointed out the trail from the ranch. As he'd promised, her stopping place was fairly close to the ranch; it looked like an easy ride.

"From the crest of that hill you'll get a fabu-lous view of the valley. It's up above the trail where the rock slide was, and you'll see some big flat rocks partway down," he told her. "It's a very gentle ride. I don't know why we haven't been that way since you guys got here, but Gary's wanted me to stick to trails going the other direction. Anyway, I like this trail and I think it's an ideal one for you to take."

As Julie sat beside him on the bale of straw with the warmth of his body so close to hers, she felt the last of her anxiety fade away. There was nothing to fear. Maggie was a surefooted and intelligent horse, and Julie knew that Nick would make certain there were no equipment

problems this time. The trail she was taking
could hardly be less dangerous or threatening.
And it was a glorious sunny day. Julie was certain that she was going to have a wonderful ride.

Chapter

Eighteen

Perched astride Maggie, Julie gazed around at the serene countryside as they meandered through pastureland and crossed a little stream that she guessed was connected to the larger one running through the valley. In the far distance she could see snow on the mountains. Amazing, considering it's July, she thought. But those craggy peaks weren't her destination.

By the time she reached the top of the hill she was heading for, the sun was high in the sky. She got out the blanket that was tied behind the saddle and opened up her lunch. As she began to eat Julie realized that she'd been so engrossed in the beauty around her that she'd forgotten to listen for Nick. She'd been sure she'd be able to tell if he was nearby, but for all she knew, he'd come and checked on her several times without her even noticing.

Partway down the other side of the hill were
the big flat rocks Nick had mentioned. Julie
could see them from where she sat and they
looked inviting, their surfaces dappled by sun-
light, partially shaded by big trees. She decided
to go down there as soon as she finished lunch.
It wasn't part of the route Nick had mapped out
for her, but it would be fun to explore on her
own. She wouldn't be in any danger—she could
turn back before she reached the canyon that
had been blocked by the rock slide.

A little shudder ran through Julie at the memory of that terrifying moment—was it only last
week?—when the canyon wall rained boulders
in her path. But she banished it, imagining herself stretched out on one of those sunny slabs
below, looking up through the trees to the
endless-seeming sky.

When she got down to the flat rocks, Julie tied
Maggie's reins to a tree limb and looked around.
It was really a beautiful spot. As she spread her
blanket her eye was caught by a small cave a
short distance away. At least she thought it was
a cave. The opening looked kind of raw, as if
the tumble of rocks below it had been covering
the mouth of the cave until last night's rain
washed them away.

She walked toward the cave and climbed over

the heap of rubble in front of it. She peered into the shadowed hollow. The partially decomposed face of a dead woman looked back at her.

Julie screamed and stumbled back toward the flat rock and Maggie, retching as she went. It was the most horrible sight she'd ever seen. Looking at bodies on TV and in the movies was one thing, but in real life . . . One arm had been chewed at by some animal. Her stomach churned, and suddenly she bent over and threw up her lunch.

Unwillingly Julie turned her head and glanced toward the cave and its dreadful contents. Waves of fear washed over her. Even though the body had obviously been dead for a while, she couldn't help feeling that danger was all around. Blindly she grabbed at Maggie's reins and scrambled up on the horse. I've got to get out of here, she thought.

"Maggie, go home!" Julie yelled to the startled horse. "Go home!"

Just as Nick had promised, those magic words sent the horse flying toward the ranch. Julie clung to the saddle horn as Maggie's long black mane snapped back in her face and stung her eyes. Julie didn't care. She didn't give a thought to the fact that they were racing across countryside that she'd carefully picked her way through on the outward trip. All she wanted to do was get away, to erase that ghastly sight from her memory.

Gary was sitting outside the barn, polishing the silver on his good saddle as Maggie came galloping up. The horse's mouth was frothing and its eyes rolled nervously. And as Julie slid down to the ground her face was just as disheveled and wild looking.

"There's a dead woman up there," she gasped to Gary. Her arm swung out, gesturing toward the cave in the hills. "We've got to call the police or something. It's terrible!"

"Are you sure she's dead?" Gary asked, sounding unnaturally calm.

Julie's hand flew to her mouth. "Oh, yes," she cried. "I saw her in this little cave and—oh, something had eaten part of her arm. . . . " She burst into sobs.

"Now, now," Gary said, and awkwardly patted her arm. "Look, you're all upset. Why don't you unsaddle Maggie and turn her loose in the corral? She needs to calm down, and so do you. I'll take care of calling the sheriff."

Julie nodded dumbly. Gary turned and walked toward the ranch house, his gait measured and a look of intense concentration on his face.

After fumbling with the cinch strap, Julie yanked the saddle off her horse's back and dumped it on the ground. Then she took Maggie's reins and led her to the corral on the far side of the barn. She opened the corral gate and pushed Maggie inside, slipping off the bridle at the last minute and latching the gate securely. Walking back to where the saddle lay in the dirt, she picked it up.

She knew she was operating on automatic pilot. Who cared if the saddle got put away properly or not? But she had to keep moving. Any activity was better than being still and letting that nightmarish face invade her mind again.

Julie lugged the heavy saddle into the barn and hoisted it on its stand in the tack room. She stopped for a moment, breathing heavily from the exertion, and then a small rustling movement in the far corner caught her eye. Gingerly she went over to investigate.

It was the barn cat's kittens. All five of them were up and waddling around on their small furry paws. "Oh, you're so cute," Julie said softly as she knelt down and touched them. The mama cat appeared out of nowhere and rubbed against Julie's thigh. "These are really pretty babies you've got," Julie told her. It was such a relief to see something so normal and full of life that she burst into tears again.

The sounds of Julie's sobs covered the slight noise Gary made as he stole up behind her, a rock clutched in his hand. Julie didn't even turn around as he lifted it above her head and smashed it down hard.

Walking quickly toward the barn door, Gary paused near the entrance and pulled a box of matches from his pants pocket. He struck three of them, dropping each of the burning sticks into mounds of loose straw on the floor of the barn.

Then, after waiting a moment to make sure they caught, he moved out of the barn and closed the big double doors with a slam. He dropped the crossbar into its brackets, securing the door shut, then he trotted back toward the ranch house. It was lucky that the barn was so far from the house, he thought. Even if it burned to the ground, it was unlikely the house would catch fire, too. And he'd been wanting to build a new barn anyway. Mrs. Fremont's money would take care of that with no problem.

Julie's first conscious thought was that her face didn't need washing. Then she realized she was lying on the barn floor and the cat was licking her, running its scratchy tongue over Julie's eyelids and cheeks.

Fighting against the overwhelming pain in her head, she struggled to her feet and staggered toward the front of the barn. The building was filling up with smoke. "It's on fire!" she suddenly said aloud. The straw on one side of the door was a crackling blaze, but Julie edged around it and shoved at the big double doors.

At first she couldn't believe it. The doors wouldn't budge. Then in a flash of understanding, she knew what had happened. Someone had knocked her out and then set the barn on fire, trapping her inside. The doors must be latched on the other side.

Only one person could have done that. Gary. He was the only person around. But why? she asked herself. Then she shook her head, and winced at the stabs of pain. No time for wondering now. She had to get out.

Julie looked around for some implement to break open the doors. But this was a sturdily built structure and no shovel or pitchfork was going to make a dent in them. She moved clumsily away from the main part of the fire, back toward the tack room, where the steep narrow stairway led up to the hayloft overhead. Maybe she should go up and try to get out that way. Surely that little door on the front of the barn's second story that they used for loading hay into the loft was unlocked.

She snatched an empty feed sack from the stack near the tack room and plunged it into a bucket of water. The smoke was thicker now and Julie was coughing violently.

Clapping the wet cloth over her nose and mouth, she headed again for the stairs. But before she'd gone even halfway up, she could see the glow of flames. The fire had spread to the hayloft.

Gagging and choking, Julie looked around wildly. There had to be a way out. She staggered back through the tack room and heard the plaintive cry of the mother cat. The poor creature had one of her kittens in her mouth, but she didn't know how to get out either. And even if she could, Julie realized, she'd have to sacrifice the other kittens. She couldn't carry out more than one.

Julie snatched up another feed sack and shook it open. With a determination she didn't know she possessed, she said, "Come on, kitty. I'm going to get all of us out of here." Kneeling, she scooped up the small furry bodies and dropped them carefully in the sack. Then she grabbed the mama cat and stuffed her in with her babies.

Holding the neck of the sack of cats in one hand and the wet cloth over her mouth with the other, Julie stood in the middle of the blazing barn. Why don't barns ever have windows? she thought irrelevantly.

Then her eyes fastened on the small tractor that was stored in the barn when it wasn't being used to move heavy stuff around the ranch. She'd walked around it so many times that she no longer even noticed it. Was it possible the keys were in the ignition?

They were, but the metal seat was hot to the touch when Julie climbed up and sat in it. If that gas tank explodes, I'm a dead person, she thought. But if you don't get out of here soon, you're a dead person anyway, she said to herself.

Julie had never driven a tractor before, but she'd have to make it work—there was no other solution. By the time the barn walls had burned open, she would be nothing more than a piece of charred meat. She perched the bag of kittens in her lap and turned the key in the ignition. With relief she heard the rackety engine sputter and cough and then roar into life.

The tractor was pointed toward the side wall of the barn. Okay, let's go, she thought desperately. It's now or never. She shoved the machine into gear and stomped hard on the accelerator. The tractor lurched forward and slammed into the barn wall. There was an earsplitting tearing sound as the wooden wall shattered.

Above the noise of the tractor's engine she could hear voices. "Where's Julie?" Nick was yelling, while Gary shouted back, "I don't know!"

Then she was past the corner of the burning barn, and they both whirled and stared at the slowly chugging tractor.

Nick began running toward her. "Julie! Are you all right?"

Gary stood stock-still, his eyes riveted on Julie. His face was slack, in the same expression of shocked surprise that he'd had yesterday when he saw her coming back on Nick's horse. In that split second Julie knew that the fall that had almost sent her over the edge of Diablo Canyon was no accident. Gary had arranged it all.

As Nick neared the tractor Julie leaped off and ran to meet him, still clutching the sackful of cats. "Oh, Nick," she cried as he caught her in his arms. "It was Gary. He tried to kill me!"

They both looked toward where Gary had been standing, but the man wasn't there any longer. Just then Hannah came galloping up behind them. "You can see the smoke for miles," she called breathlessly. "Where's the fire department?"

"Probably Gary didn't call them," Julie said shakily.

"Well, maybe the phones are down and he's gone to get help," Hannah told them. "I just saw him leave in the Jeep." Then Hannah registered Julie's soot-blackened face. "What happened to you?" she asked, and jumped down from her horse.

But Julie ignored the other girl's question. On some other level her mind had been running through the strange incidents that had happened since they all arrived at the K Bar K Ranch. Now the pieces suddenly fell into place.

"He's gone to kill Josh!" She knew it was true, but there was no time to explain to the others. "We've got to stop him!"

Nick and Hannah stared at Julie in disbelief, and she felt a spurt of anger. Why didn't they understand? But she couldn't waste any more time—Gary had a head start and somebody had to save Josh.

Julie turned and ran for the minivan. Then Nick came up behind her and caught her arm. "We'll take my truck, it's faster."

CHAPTER

NINETEEN

The pickup's rust spots and the dent along one side belied the smooth power under its hood. But Julie's hands were clenched tight in her lap as she willed the truck to go even faster. How far ahead of them was Gary by now? Had he already completed his deadly purpose? No, she thought fiercely, the image of Josh lying helpless in his hospital bed clear in her mind's eye.

A fire engine screamed past them, heading toward the ranch. I guess someone called them, Julie thought dispassionately, maybe a neighbor saw the smoke. It didn't seem to matter now—all she could think about was the man who was closing in on her friend.

Nick swerved around a corner and slammed on the brakes in front of the hospital entrance. Almost before the truck had stopped, Julie was out and through the glass doors. Ignoring the elevator, she hurriedly scanned the lobby and then ran toward the door marked STAIRS. Nick was right behind her, and they pounded up to the second floor.

As they burst into the corridor Julie's breath caught in her throat. She could see the nurse moving around in the other intensive-care room, her back to the glass wall. And in Josh's room a looming figure stood beside the bed, bending over the carrot-haired head on the pillow.

"No!" Julie's scream echoed along the hall. Then she was running again, past the nurses' station, and throwing herself against the door to Josh's room. "Leave him alone!"

Gary straightened abruptly. Wheeling away from the bed, he took a menacing step toward Julie. His strong hands reached out to grab her. She tried to tear them away as his fingers closed around her neck.

"Let go of her, Gary!" Nick's tall form seemed to fill the doorway, and the man's grip loosened in confusion. Julie wrenched herself away and circled around to take up a protective stance on the other side of the bed.

"All of you, out of here, right now!" The nurse's commanding voice left no room for argument. She shoved past Nick and confronted Gary, glaring at him sternly. "I said now!"

Caught in the sweeping gale of her anger, Nick backed out into the hall, and Gary moved slowly after him, his face still blank with shock. After a moment Julie followed them, while the nurse turned her attention to Josh.

Time seemed to stop as the three of them stood immobile, a frozen tableau. At last Gary broke the spell. His heavy footsteps thudded as he charged toward the stairway door.

Nick raced after him and grabbed his arm, and the big man, off balance, fell to the floor. As he struggled to get up, two men appeared at the top of the stairs. One, who was wearing a guard's uniform, stepped forward and put a restraining hand on Nick's arm. "What's going on here?"

Julie burst into speech. "This man"—she gestured at Gary—"tried to kill me, he hit me over the head and started a fire in the barn. And now he tried to kill Josh!"

The guard looked dubious. "Well, now, miss, that's a pretty serious—"

"It's true! You have to believe me!" Julie stared down at the man on the floor, her eyes blazing. "Tell him, Gary! Just tell him what you tried to do to me, and to Josh."

Gary lowered his eyes and made no reply. But his defeated expression and slumped shoulders were almost an admission of guilt. The guard gazed at him for a moment, and then said to the orderly who had accompanied him, "Jim, call the cops."

Driving back to the ranch with Nick, Julie was astonished to realize that only an hour had gone by since they'd arrived at the hospital. She was exhausted. She'd told her story at least three times, to various official people and finally to the sheriff. But now two deputies were following them to the ranch to talk to Mrs. Fremont and Ilene, and another group was going on horseback to bring down the body from the cave.

Hannah met them at the ranch-house door, looking harried and relieved to see them. "I'm so glad to see you," she said. "Where have you been?" She looked questioningly at the two deputies and then went on, "I'm awfully worried. I can't find Mrs. Fremont, I don't know where she's gone, and Ilene is acting really weird."

One of the deputies said, "I think we'd better talk to Ilene."

"Okay," Hannah told him uncertainly. She led the way to Mrs. Fremont's room. "She's in here."

She opened the door, and they all filed in quietly. It took a moment for Julie's eyes to adjust to the darkened room, but when they did, she saw a neatly made bed with no one in it. Then Hannah grabbed her arm and pointed. On the floor in the corner beyond the bed, a woman was huddled facing the wall. It was Ilene.

The shorter deputy said, "Ilene? Ilene, where's Mrs. Fremont?"

But the woman stared stonily at the wall, her eyes not even flickering in his direction.

With a glance at the deputy, Nick sat on the edge of Mrs. Fremont's bed and spoke quietly to the woman crouched on the floor in the corner. "I'm sorry, Ilene," Nick told her. "Gary's been arrested. He tried to kill Julie." He touched her on the shoulder. "Maybe you'd better tell us now what's been going on."

Suddenly the woman's angular form began to shake with big, racking sobs. "I told him it wouldn't work," she cried. "I told him we'd never get away with it."

Julie and Hannah retreated to the bedroom doorway openmouthed. Brian, Bret, and Roy had seen the deputies' car pull up and now they crowded in to listen. They all stood speechless in horror as Ilene spilled out the story.

It seemed that Gary had gotten into an argument with Mrs. Fremont several weeks before.

"He's always had kind of a temper," Ilene said sadly. "I knew it would get him into trouble one day. That and his get-rich-quick schemes."

Before he knew what he'd done, Gary had clobbered the older woman over the head and killed her. Julie heard the in-drawn breaths of amazement and shock from the other kids, and suddenly realized that they didn't yet know about the body she'd found in the cave. She was shocked, too, but not completely surprised, to learn that the body was that of Mrs. Fremont.

Ilene's voice went on in a monotone, saying that Gary had come up with a plan. He'd hide Mrs. Fremont's body up in the mountains and they'd go on pretending that the woman was still living at the ranch.

There was no time to stop the teenagers from coming to the ranch. It was an annual custom and Gary didn't want to raise questions by trying to cancel the two-week stint. Instead he had convinced Ilene that she could impersonate Mrs. Fremont whenever it was necessary. She'd done such a good job that even the banker had been fooled and had handed over access to Mrs. Fremont's accounts to Gary and Ilene.

Gary's plan had been to tell everyone that Mrs. Fremont was going on a long trip and then to siphon off as much money from the ranch accounts as he could. Ilene wanted to run away, but Gary was sure they could stay on at the ranch indefinitely.

"And it might have even worked if that nosy boy hadn't ruined things," Ilene wailed. Although Julie guessed what was coming, she winced in agony as Ilene described how Josh had discovered their charade and started asking questions. Gary had had no choice but to kill him, the woman explained. But he hadn't hit him hard enough.

Even though she knew what must be coming next, Julie felt her hands turn icy cold as Ilene continued. Gary was certain that Julie knew what Josh had discovered; she'd become a threat to his plans. And then she'd accidentally found Mrs. Fremont's body, so once again Gary had had no choice.

Raising her eyes, Ilene looked beseechingly at Julie. "I never wanted to kill you," she wailed. Tears began rolling down her cheeks.

Julie stared back at the woman, unable to summon any response. Then she felt Hannah's arm around her waist. "Come on, Julie," the other girl said quietly.

As they walked together through the living room Julie heard one of the deputies say, "Ilene, I think you'd better come into town with us."

By mutual consent the two girls went outside into the warm sunshine, putting the darkened room and its terrifying revelations behind them. At Hannah's urging, Julie told her everything that had happened from the moment she'd discovered Mrs. Fremont's body to Gary's arrest in town.

"Incredible," Hannah said, shaking her head. "I always thought Gary was a creep, but I couldn't have imagined anything like this." She paused and then went on, "Of course I didn't know anything about the cave or how the fire started or what Gary was planning when he drove off. I had no idea why you and Nick took off."

"We saw the fire truck heading this way," Julie told her.

"Oh, yeah, things were pretty exciting for a while. They couldn't save the barn, but at least all the horses are okay—we turned them loose. By tomorrow morning they'll probably come on home."

"Oh!" The mention of the horses jogged Julie's memory. "The kittens!"

Hannah gave a slightly shaky laugh. "Right, it was kind of a surprise when I found that sack. But don't worry, they're fine. I put them in our room on a blanket."

The telephone rang inside the house. After a moment Nick poked his head out the dining-room door. "Julie, it's for you."

Surprised, Julie went inside. When she returned, all the guys were hanging around, re-running the startling chain of events they'd all been through. "That was the doctor," Julie told them with a grin. "He wanted to let us know that Josh is okay—in fact, he's being moved out of intensive care tomorrow. And his parents are arriving sometime tonight."

"Great!" Brian and Bret said in unison.

"It's about time something good happened for a change," Roy added.

By dinnertime Lucinda had returned, her mother recovered, and Nick had arranged for his mom to come and stay overnight at the ranch. They all hung around by the fire in the living room until late in the evening, drawing comfort from Etta's cheery presence. Nick was going to stay over, too, sleeping in Josh's bed. But when Etta offered to share the girls' room, Julie and Hannah politely declined. They'd been through so much together, and the thought of the older woman, nice as she was, intruding in the bond they'd formed wasn't appealing to either of them.

Hannah and Julie sat on the edges of their

beds, sipping at the mugs of hot chocolate that Etta had urged them to take.

"I know what Roy's been up to," Hannah said finally.

Julie looked at her in surprise. "How'd you find out?"

Hannah laughed. "I asked him. It was as simple as that. It was mostly Josh he didn't want to find out. He was afraid Josh would make a big deal out of it and tell everyone. But I guess he thinks I'm the sympathetic type, so he told me. And it turns out that he told Nick when we first got here. I never could figure out why Nick didn't seem to notice that Roy was missing, and now I know. Nick had given Roy his word that he wouldn't say anything, and he kept it."

"Well, don't keep me in suspense any longer," Julie said. "What's Roy's big secret?"

"He can't read," Hannah told her. "Well, actually he's learning. That's what he was doing at the library. A lady there works with the local literacy group and she's been helping him."

Julie looked at Hannah. "That's incredible," she said. "I mean, you hear about people who can't read, but Roy's our age. How's he managed to get through school?"

"I'm sure it hasn't been easy. In fact, I think part of the reason he finally admitted he had a problem was that it's been getting more and more difficult for him to hide it. And he's a smart guy. He wants to go to college."

Julie shook her head slowly. "No wonder he acts so prickly sometimes." Then she said, "Now something Josh told me makes sense. He said he found a little kid's book in Roy's stuff. I guess Roy must have been using it to practice."

"Probably so," Hannah agreed.

They were both lost in thought for a moment. "Do you suppose he'd like to read that book aloud to the kids tomorrow at the shelter?" Hannah asked at last.

"Gosh, I don't know," Julie told her. "I wouldn't want to embarrass him."

"Well, he's got a lot to be proud of. And it's not like we're all friends of his from school or anything. He'll probably never see any of us again after we leave on Saturday."

"Let's ask him tomorrow," Julie suggested. "The worst he can say is no." She looked across at Hannah. "Does that mean that we'll never see each other again either after Saturday?"

Hannah shook her head and laughed. "Oh, no. I'm already making plans."